Heart
OF THE
FUTURE

ROBIN BRANDE

HEART OF THE FUTURE
Heart-warming Stories of Love, Courage, and Compassion in a
Not-so-distant Future
By Robin Brande

Published by Ryer Publishing
www.ryerpublishing.com
© 2025 Robin Brande
www.robinbrande.com
All rights reserved.
Cover art by grandfailure/Deposit Photos
Ebook ISBN: 978-1-952383-75-5
Paperback ISBN: 978-1-952383-76-2

"Time Map" was first published in *Pulphouse Magazine* #20.

All rights reserved. No part of this book may be reproduced in any form or by any electronic or mechanical means, including information storage and retrieval systems, without written permission from the author, except for the use of brief quotations in a book review.

This is a work of fiction. Any references to historical events, real people, or real locales are used fictitiously. Other names, characters, places, and incidents are the product of the author's imagination, and any resemblance to actual events or locales or persons, living or dead, is entirely coincidental.

No part of this book may be used or reproduced in any manner for the purpose of training artificial intelligence technologies or systems.

ALSO BY ROBIN BRANDE

Winnie Parsons Mysteries

A Mind for Mysteries (Collection)

The Genius Track

A Man of Appetites

A Drop of Sweat

The Long Gray Hook

The Slip of a Rib

The Cabin Ghost

The Secret Juror

The Truth Chamber

Dove Season Universe

Dove Season

Finder

Seeker

Believer

Maker

Explorer

<u>Young Adult</u>

Evolution, Me & Other Freaks of Nature

Fat Cat

Doggirl

Replay

Into the Parallel

Caught in the Parallel

Seize the Parallel

Beyond the Parallel

Book of Earth

Book of Water

<u>Romance</u>

Love Proof

Freefall

Heart of Ice

Fire and Ice

<u>Self-Help</u>

What If You're Doing It Right?

What If You're Doing It Right? For Teens

<u>Collections</u>

The Love of a Good Dog

Mountain Tough

The Miraculous Unknown

Life with the Afterlife

Heart of the Future

CONTENTS

Heart OF THE FUTURE

HUMANS' NATURE

1

————————————

Wood and stone were soothing to the soul. But they weren't efficient. They weren't functional.

At least that's what Dary's supervisor said.

Only the specialized metals were light enough for transport. There would be no natural materials. Too heavy. Too expensive, fuel-wise.

Her supervisor, Mr. Marsh, had shown Dary around the facility six months ago. It was as modern as any place she had ever seen. A large manufacturing floor. Fifty worktables set up in two rows. Everything very clean. Bright. Sterile. The tiling on the floor was new. Dary could still smell the adhesives and the synthetic coating.

Mr. Marsh was very proud of the workspace, as he

should have been. It meant his company had passed all the rigors of bidding and competition. After two years of tense waiting, he finally received word that it was a go. He was the one.

Dary was secondary.

She had a reputation, of sorts. A good honest worker. Gave a full day's work and then some. Was a problem solver. A team player. All the recommendations you'd want to see for a girl only twenty. What did she know. But she was good, within her limits. Everybody said.

"Here are your supplies," Mr. Marsh told her the first day she arrived at the workspace. She would have her very own large steel-topped table, no one to share it with. That alone was an improvement.

At school, Dary stood shoulder to shoulder with eight other students every time she needed to work. It was why she did her designs at home, pencil on paper, old style. Feeling her way through.

Everyone else—everyone—used the latest computer programs and graphics. Their designs looked sleek and perfect. Always so perfect.

Dary's were messy. Too organic, her professors cautioned. Not practical. Not here, not anymore.

Mr. Marsh gave her a full-body workshop apron, a lovely pine green, with two deep pockets in front. Dary slipped it over her head and tied it behind her waist. The apron was for someone much taller, but she didn't mind the feel of it hanging all the way down below her shins. It was official. Professional. She was a maker.

Mr. Marsh pointed to the screen mounted on a hydraulic arm just above her worktable. That way she could pull it toward her, push it away, twist it, turn it so she could see it no matter what she was doing and where she worked at her assigned station. "There's the list of what we need," Mr. Marsh told her. "I'm counting on you. We're already behind."

"Yes, sir." Dary tied back her dark hair. Tightened the bow on the apron strings at the back. Watched Mr. Marsh go on to the next worktable where another student from the Craftsmen Academy waited for his instructions.

I'm on my own, Dary thought.

Finally.

2

At the Academy the professors taught innovations. It made sense. The world was not what it was fifty years ago, they reminded everyone, as if anyone had to say it.

Trees were a fond memory. When the water dried up, it was humans first, livestock second, plants a distant third or fourth or more.

Livestock first, pets second. So they were the next to go.

Dary knew the history. She knew it too well. She loved the old books with their nostalgic pictures. People tended to move on. It was too sad, too tragic, too difficult. True. But it was so beautiful, that past. Full of life and greenery, full of forests and jungles and wildlife. Now green was a manufactured color. The smell of pine trees and maple sap were replicated and bottled. You could buy a substitute for moss by the sheet, like it was fabric. Same with grass if you wanted it around your house or even inside it. Lay it down in squares, squish your toes into it. Doesn't that feel nice?

But no one dared to say, *Don't you miss it?* What was the point of that?

Dary's parents couldn't afford the richest upgrades. Someone gave her a little book when she was four or five with squares of things she could touch: this was leather. This was fur. These were feathers. Feel them. This was what a fern frond used to be like. Isn't it strange?

Like listening to recordings of bird song. That was her mother's favorite. Nights next to the player listening to some broadcast from a century before when a woman played her cello out in her garden and a nightingale sang along.

Just stories, maybe. Everything could be made. Sounds, textures, colors. When she was little Dary used to ask her parents, "Is this real?" when they showed her something in a book or on a recording. It was hard to tell what was made or what was truly a part of the past.

"If you can see it, it's real," her father would say. And often he added, "If you can make it, even better."

He was a weather forecaster at one time in his life, before Dary was born. Then there was very little weather to talk about. Always the same: dry, windy, dusty, hot. Not much call for nuance after awhile. He gave up his job. No point to it.

They lived in what was left of the woods near what was left of a lake in the small town of Star Lake, Wisconsin.

For a while, only a short while after Dary came along, her father still found bits of wood to make things with. He treasured them. Never wasted them. When they were gone, there would be no more to take their place.

He made Dary little carvings. Little toys. A box, large enough to fit five books lying flat side by side, and with a small thin secret drawer along its base that you only knew was there because someone showed you.

In the extravagance of her tenth birthday, he made her a real bookcase, a cabinet three shelves high, with a glass front made from glass he salvaged from a window in their little house. He said it wasn't a good view out of it anyway, and boarded it up. But Dary knew it was just so he could make her this one last beautiful thing.

After he died, Dary took a moment every day to open the glass door and stick her head in and breathe in the scent of wood. She knew that over time that smell would fade, but she wanted to savor it as long as she could.

This is real, he taught her. Wood and stone, water, trees, grass. All real. *I'm so sorry you missed it.*

But the skills he taught her still worked. How to

design useful things. How to make them as beautiful as you can, even if it's just to please yourself. Even if it's just to lift your own heart. Because other people will be lifted, too, even if they don't understand why.

Dary studied the list on the screen above her worktable. None of the items were hard. She was just another worker. Some things still needed a human touch. Design ideas were still useful. Problem solving was still useful.

Efficiently, practically, real. With the materials on hand. With what the world still had for its own use.

And with what was left, to fashion new furniture and equipment and living space for the people who would need them on their journey out beyond to where maybe there were still trees and water and colors and pets and birds.

The explorers. The ones who might never come back, but would be able to send messages: Yes, here. No, not there. No … not anywhere. Maybe. Nobody knew. It was just a hope and a wish. But you still had to try things, Dary knew. You still had to put in the effort. Because how would you know otherwise? You couldn't just curl up and die.

Her father taught her that. And her mother while she could. They didn't give up. Dary watched them. They both tried, all the way to the end.

How could she possibly do less?

3

Six months felt like long enough in the beginning, but as the days sped by, everyone in the workspace was feeling the panic. Mr. Marsh came in three times a day to check their progress. Never fast enough. Never good enough. More. Better. Hurry.

At night, after the overhead lights were shut off and everyone sent back to their rooms, Dary drank a slurry of coffee and black tea and sugar to stay awake and remain focused.

She sneaked out adhesives and other compounds. She made things by the light of her single desk lamp in the small room assigned to her in the row of small rooms everyone in the workspace slept in. If she slept four hours a night, it felt like too much. She could go without for now, for this short window of time when it might matter what she invented and imagined. When the project was done, she might never work again. No one could make any promises.

This was it. Her chance to make what she could make.

The finish date loomed large on the calendar on their screens. Five weeks away, now four, three.

The explorers, twenty of them, were already in isolation. They had said goodbye, maybe—probably—forever to their families and friends, and now they just waited to do what they were ready to do. For them, maybe three weeks seemed unbearably long. Let's get on with it.

There would be the unveiling. Just a private ceremony for Mr. Marsh and the workers at the workspace and the explorers. Because if anything was bad or wrong and the explorers hated it or said it wouldn't work, there was no point in having that humiliation made public. Bad enough to have your designs and your work thrown away at the last minute, your last six months a waste. Your education and your hopes a waste.

Dary sneaked more supplies back to her room every night. She built things. She tried things. Discarded bad ideas, tried again.

During the day she risked looking around at what everyone else was making. Their furnishings looked clean and sleek. Their storage containers and lighting units and useful equipment for the explorers' cabins and dining space and showers and toilet cubicles all looked top of the line and perfect. Made of the lightweight metal Mr. Marsh's company specialized in. Made with space travel in mind, practical and efficient and real.

And Dary's furnishings looked that way, too. They had to. Her shelves that turned on a spindle, where explorers could store their private supplies like eating utensils and clothing and mementos from home. That had to fit in a tight corner of a small cabin of a speedy modern ship. Everyone was mindful of the weight. Nothing extra. Nothing frivolous.

At night Dary studied pictures of old seaships, of how the cabins were arranged, where the sailors stowed everything, how they were able to live at sea for years at a time and still live good lives. Dary thought about that: about giving the explorers good lives. Even if they were short lives and the explorers were never coming back.

Like her father wasting good glass and the last of the wood to make Dary that beautiful cabinet for her tenth birthday. Maybe a hundred years from now some of it would still exist, rotting away, but still real. Real wood. A reminder of what used to be.

Dary wanted to give the explorers at least that: a reminder of what used to be. As real as she could make it in these times when the old was no longer real, but just pictures and old recordings and memories from people who were there.

One week, five days, two days.

Dary slept just a few hours a night. She could sleep later. After this project was over, what else was there for her to do but sleep?

Finally the day.

Mr. Marsh agreed everyone could make it a bit of a show. Cover their creations with synthetic tarps and remove the coverings with a flourish. Why not. Everyone worked so hard. This was it. Might as well enjoy a bit of flash.

Mr. Marsh looked as if he had given up sleeping several months ago. His face was so much thinner. His clothes hung on him like they belonged to someone twice his size. The bags under his eyes took up half his cheeks. If he survived this, Dary doubted he would survive very much longer. He had run himself to the end of his cord. Just like her father. Trying, trying, all the way to the end.

The workspace was bright with overhead lights and lights brought in for the individual worktables, to make sure everything looked as sharp and clean and perfect as possible.

Dary wheeled in her creations. Four of them, on movable stands, that she had kept hidden in her room the past few weeks while she continued working on their prototypes at her worktable as if they were what she would present.

Their small rooms, they had all been told, were roughly the same size as the cabins the explorers would travel in. So try to imagine what they needed and what could reasonably fit in there. Be practical. Be efficient.

Dary had moved the four pieces around her room, trying out various configurations. She knew what it would feel like for an explorer to be lying in bed and want to reach for something or store something. How it felt to stand within the space and feel comforted. Feel loved. Feel treasured.

Dary felt that way just from keeping the cabinet her father made. The smell of the wood. The beauty of the design and craftsmanship. The love that went into creating it and giving it to her.

It was in storage now while she waited to know where she might live next. It had been right beside her bed at the Academy, but they were told not to bring anything with them to Mr. Marsh's workspace. No room for anything but their single duffel of clothing.

But that wasn't true. Dary had seen that right away when she first arrived. She could have fit the cabinet in there and so much more. You just had to know how to design it. Which she did. She knew it and she made things.

The explorers looked worthy. Strong and noble and brave. They walked through the workspace as if they were already free of gravity. Higher, taller, more majestic than any people Dary had ever seen. Maybe it was her imagination, but the explorers looked absolutely magical. As if they never belonged on the dry, dusty earth, but had always been meant to live in the stars.

Her gut tightened the closer they came to her. She knew she had made her best. She knew it in her heart. But there was still that moment of showing people. Of worrying what they would say. It's too heavy. It isn't practical. It's beautiful, but we can't possibly take it.

But it wasn't too heavy. It was practical. Dary understood her craft.

"This is Daryann Majors," Mr. Marsh said to the explorers. Dary shook every offered hand. She still wore her long green apron. It was her uniform. She was proud of it. It was her shield and her armor. It made her feel brave.

"Before I…" She could hear her voice shake. Dary blinked hard and steadied her racing heart. Steadied her words. "Before I show you," she told the explorers, "I want you to know how much I admire you and think of you. I know you are people, not machines. I want you to love what you see every time you walk into your rooms."

Dary pulled the synthetic tarp off her first creation.

"This is your stool," she told them, although the moment she said it she knew it was obvious. But what wasn't obvious was how it would feel. She gestured to the nearest explorer, a woman who looked like she walked straight out of a book about Vikings or ancient warriors. She was tall and broad-shouldered and very serious looking. Not to be trifled with. Don't waste her time.

The woman, Major Thelkos, gave Dary a curious look, but she obliged her and sat down.

Dary wanted that expression: the look of surprise and delight. Then the *ahhhhh*....

It was all made of metal, as everyone was required, but Dary covered it with the lightest weight synthetic fabrics and gels, mixed into a compound of her own invention, something pliable and soft as air, soft as deep moss, soft as water.

Major Thelkos laughed. She *laughed*. She stood up and told the others to try. One by one, twenty of them sat on Dary's stool and all of them gave her those same looks of approval and delight and maybe even gratitude. There was some of that, she was sure. Because although her fellow Academy graduates were all superb at what they did, they were efficient and practical, and Dary was not. Not like that. She had had her share of fights with her professors, but what was life if you couldn't enjoy the things you saw and the things you had? Why shouldn't Dary still treasure that book her parents' friend gave her when she was small, the one that let her feel soft things and old things and keep alive the idea that those things mattered?

The smell of real wood in her father's cabinet mattered. It lifted Dary's heart. These were humans going off to the stars to explore and find another world.

They needed soft things and old things and beauty. They deserved that.

Dary unveiled the cabinet she had made. Metal, lightweight, with a lightweight synthetic door that Dary had made to look like glass. Glass that had been repurposed from a rundown house that still had a view of the lake, even though the lake was no longer there.

Dary had spent night after night combining synthetic fabric swatches with different adhesives and gels and compounds until she found the right combination to apply over the metal to give it the look and feel of wood.

Mr. Marsh tipped the cabinet side to side, testing, Dary knew, its weight. But it was no heavier than anything anyone else had made. It was just more real.

Dary saw one of the explorers turn his head to the side as if he didn't want anyone to see his face. But Dary saw it before he did that. She knew what he felt. She felt it, too, when she finally got the combination right.

She listened to the explorers murmuring to each other. It was as if no one wanted to say any of it directly to her. Like it was some secret delight they were afraid they might be in trouble for. As if, in this time of serious matters, serious danger, they weren't allowed to have beautiful things.

"What else?" Major Thelkos asked her quietly. As if she was reluctant to see what was under the next tarp, in case it might disappoint them. In case Dary wasn't able to keep it going, this strange gift she was offering the explorers.

Dary removed the cover.

She could see her fellow students gathered in a wreath around the explorers. An outer ring of other workers just like she was. Not important, not the way these twenty brave explorers were, no one whose names would matter fifty years from now or even one.

Dary caught the eye of the girl who used to work next to her at their worktable their first year, but who had gone on to the advanced level quickly and never bothered to speak to any of the slower students like Dary anymore.

The girl looked shocked. Maybe even a little angry. But when she locked eyes with Dary her expression softened. Because they were all in this together. They were all, actually, nobodies together. Working on this one great project and then facing the same unknown beyond it. No one knew if they had jobs tomorrow. No one knew anything. They had been working in this isolated factory for the past six months and didn't know a thing about what was going on in the world outside. That was how it was designed. Because hearing more bad news wouldn't inspire anyone, Mr. Marsh told them. So let's just be on this ship together and do our best and worry about tomorrow tomorrow.

But Dary knew that the not knowing was too harsh and too cold. And humans needed comfort. They just did. From the cavemen learning to harness fire to now, still right now, humans needed comfort and warmth and beauty. Her father knew it and Dary knew it. That was just real. That was true.

So Dary's third creation was a bed. A soft, warm bed made of materials that weighed barely anything but that were necessary for humans to feel loved. One of the men, Captain Somebody, Dary forgot his name, lay down on it first and he sighed and closed his eyes, and Dary knew that he felt it, the love she had poured into it, the way she had thought about all of them and about what they needed to feel right at the end of the day. To feel human, not like machines that the world had launched into space to save them.

The explorers took turns, some of them impatiently nudging each other to move along. In between turns Mr. Marsh lifted one end of the bed to test its weight. "Remarkable," she heard him mutter.

He hadn't said a word to her yet, not directly. But Dary watched his face, listened to him accepting explorers' compliments, and she knew he still doubted her until he tested the weights every time, but then it was all right. He believed.

"What's this last thing?" Major Thelkos asked her. "Come on," she said with a smile. "Show us."

Dary had noticed the postures of the explorers. They had been upright and tense, brave and noble when they came into the workspace. But now they were more relaxed. Not so rock hard. More pliable. More comfortable.

Happier.

Where they were going would be hard enough. Why suffer along the way?

"This is for your treasures," Dary said, unveiling the last creation.

She had copied it from a pinecone. The way every individual section of it looked like a small shelf, paddle-shaped, and tilted ever so slightly upward, giving the whole storage unit a rounded shape. She spun it on its base to show them how it moved.

She used her brown synthetic fabrics and adhesives and gels to give it the same dark brown color and texture of a pinecone. Mr. Marsh ran his fingers along one of the shelves. It had the smooth bumps and ridges of a pinecone, but also a little tackiness to it, to keep items in place. Like pine sap, but without leaving any sticky residue. Dary had worked many nights over many weeks to get that just right.

She took a photo out of its slim sleeve that protected it inside her apron pocket. She stuck it to the outside lip of one of the shelves. A memento to greet her every time she returned to her room. A way for the explorers to see their families and friends and old beloved pets without adding any weight for frames or needing to call up the pictures on their screens. They could have the pictures there all the time to remember why they left, what was worth saving.

No one asked her who the man and woman in the photo were. Everyone lost so many, there was no point in asking anymore. No one's story was any more tragic than anyone else's.

But Dary looked at her parents now, smiling on the shore of the lake, and she drank in the beauty of the trees that surrounded them and the grasses that grew back then. None of it was real anymore, but what Dary made now, for these explorers, was as real as she could manage. To give them comfort and beauty and a reminder of the natural world humans once loved and would love to experience again.

Maybe on another planet. Maybe in fifty years or a hundred. Maybe long after Dary had left this one behind.

But it was worth remembering—no, it was essential. Practical. Necessary to remember—what the real world used to look like and feel like and smell like. It was why Dary brushed on several coats of the best imitation she could make of what pine used to smell like. Please remember. Please find this. It matters. Humans need this.

Before they left her workstation, more hands were offered this time than when they first arrived. Twenty handshakes. Twenty pairs of eyes meeting her eyes, gazes of appreciation and acknowledgment. They got it.

They understood why she had made them what she made. That was all the recognition Dary needed—from them, the humans she made them for, the people she wanted to bring comfort and beauty to even though they had left this world far behind.

When it was all over, and everyone had displayed their creations, and the explorers made their speeches and Mr. Marsh made his, Dary carefully covered her pieces of furniture again and began wheeling the largest of them out of the workspace.

"Wait," the girl from the advanced level, Rachel, told her. "Can I?"

Dary's gut tightened again. She knew her work was good, but her fellow students could sometimes be mean. Rachel had been mean. Why end the day with that instead of with the good, warm feeling Dary had right now?

"Please," Rachel said. She looked nervous, not her usual confident, arrogant self. "It looks … amazing."

Dary gave in. She couldn't think of a way not to. And a part of her … wanted to hear. Wanted the praise from one more person. She had to admit that.

She watched Rachel remove the tarp and lie down on the bed. Rachel closed her eyes, just like that explorer did. But no sigh. No smile. No expression at all.

Rachel swung her legs over the sides. "Thanks." She stood up and walked away.

Dary watched her go, wondering what went wrong.

Out of the corner of her eye she saw movement on the bed. Someone else lying down to test it.

Mr. Marsh.

He did not jump up right away. Not like Rachel. He closed his eyes and lay there, perfectly still, for all of a minute. Maybe longer.

When he did rise, he lifted the nearest end to test its weight again. Still light. Maybe he didn't really believe it before, but he had to this time.

"Come see me tomorrow," he told her.

"I … thought we had to leave. The bus is coming first thing."

"They're leaving," Mr. Marsh said. "Not you."

Dary wheeled the bed back to her room. Then the pinecone shelving unit, then the cabinet, and the stool.

Each time she came back for one, she found her fellow workers trying it out, touching the surfaces, sniffing, lifting.

Dary noticed that Rachel was already gone. She had left her work behind at her station, although many of the others were doing what Dary was, bringing them back to their rooms. Mr. Marsh said they could enjoy them tonight. The explorers were sending him a list tomorrow of everything they approved and wanted. He would then quickly manufacture twenty each of all of them in time for the launch.

Everyone else's plans were simple and could be made

by any machines on Mr. Marsh's floor. Dary's were more complicated than that. Maybe that was why he told her to stay. She had to explain all the strange things she did to make the strange things she made.

But in the morning, after the buses had come and hauled everyone else away, Dary came back into the workspace to meet with Mr. Marsh at the time he said.

Major Thelkos was there. So were several other explorers. Dary waited off to the side until they were done with their conversation.

But Major Thelkos saw her there, back in the corner near bins full of fasteners and braces and metal tubes and metal sheets and everything else the workers had used to cobble together their pieces.

Major Thelkos motioned for Dary to come join them.

She had a list. Handwritten, just like the old days. The way Dary liked to make lists of her own.

Major Thelkos showed it to Dary.

"Can you make all of these, too?"

The same items that her fellow workers had already unveiled yesterday. Toilets and tables, chairs, shelves, lighting fixtures, storage units—the list was so long it made Dary's heart pound.

"Not … in time," Dary said. Her voice shook. She was scared but didn't want to show it. Not to these brave women and men.

"But you can," said Mr. Marsh. "Can't you, Daryann."

He so rarely used her name. Dary hesitated, but then nodded.

"It's a long trip," said Major Thelkos. "We made a decision." She looked around at her fellow explorers. "All of us. We'd rather delay our launch a little longer. It's worth it. We want you to make everything we need."

Dary stared at her in awe. Not possible. Not real.

"We'll work quickly," Mr. Marsh promised. Dary wondered how much of him would be left when they were done. He was already disappearing. Already running himself into the ground.

But these were the times, and it must be done. Her parents knew it, Dary knew it.

What else was the human race to do but to work hard for each other, to help?

"I can make them," Dary said.

She had to be strong. For everyone.

And she had to be soft for them, too. To care. To make things that were beautiful and lifted the hearts of the bravest humans willing to leave the Earth.

She pulled her apron over her head and tightened the straps in back.

Time to work.

THE REFUGEES

1

____

They're so small.

Jonna had seen some of them from further away, but it was different looking at one of them up close.

A three-foot mother pushing her baby in a human stroller, the stroller the size a toddler might use to push her doll. The alien baby no bigger than a Coke bottle, his or her head the largest part of the form, like an inverted bowling pin.

Wrapped in a blue baby blanket. A donation from someone kind.

Jonna smiled at the woman. The mother. Maybe they weren't called women where they came from. So much still wasn't known. It came in only bits and pieces.

Hungry, the thought came now.

"Yes," Jonna said out loud to the mother. "Let me show you where to go."

The monastery was a maze. Jonna had taken her first tour of it this morning, her first day of volunteering, and now she couldn't swear she remembered where everything was.

Built in the 1940s on twenty acres of land between Albuquerque and Santa Fe, the monastery had been empty for the past several years for reasons Jonna didn't quite understand. A developer had bought it a few months ago, intending to tear it down and build a gated community on the twenty acres.

But then the Crisis occurred. The aliens arrived in droves. And for whatever reason, whether it was his secretly charitable heart or the lure of tax credits or as a way to appease the various groups objecting to his demolition, the developer decided to allow one of the charities to turn the monastery into temporary housing for the aliens who had been processed by a specially created immigration division.

The developer's offer was for only six months. After that he would go forward with his subdivision plans. His opponents relented. Everyone understood the great need.

"We're getting anywhere from a hundred to three hundred refugees a day," the volunteer coordinator, Marilyn, told Jonna as she showed her around.

"A *day?*" Jonna repeated. She gazed around the outdoor courtyard at the crowd of grayish aliens, so silent and polite.

There was no pushing here, no shoving, no crying, except by the volunteers. Marilyn showed Jonna the rooms set aside on each of the three floors, specifically for that.

"You're going to want to break down," Marilyn said. "It's natural. I've been doing this for three months now, and I still cry at least two or three times a day. It's impossible not to. Just accept that. But try not to do it in front of them. They really seem to feel it. Try to make it to one of the crying rooms."

She motioned Jonna on, past the outdated but clean-looking kitchen, to the large open area next door.

Whatever it had been before in its religious life, the room was now a communal sleeping area filled with rows of small blue cots. Each cot held a small pillow on one end and a brightly-colored fleece blanket on the other. A child-sized backpack sat in the center.

It was the sight of the baby cribs, though, about a dozen of them lined along one wall, that brought a lump to Jonna's chest. She could feel it rising into her throat.

Marilyn must have known it, had probably seen it hundreds of times with new volunteers, because she reached over then and gave Jonna's arm an encouraging squeeze. "We appreciate you coming here. They appreciate it, too. All of it. Thank you."

Jonna nodded, blinking away tears. She cleared her throat and turned from the doorway and continued following Marilyn on the tour.

"Infirmary here," Marilyn said, pointing as she walked briskly past another door. "One on each floor. A lot of the refugees come in sick or injured."

"Injured how?" Jonna asked.

"Some of them from the crashes," Marilyn said. "Some from ARC. Don't get me started. I'm not a violent person, but those people could change my mind."

ARC was the special immigration division created to deal with the Crisis. Alien Refugee Command.

Jonna understood Marilyn's anger. She had had the same reaction the day before. It was why she finally realized that just donating clothing wasn't enough.

"Let's go up to the second floor," Marilyn said. She began trotting up the stairs.

But Jonna was still at the foot of them, staring at a series of photocopied faces taped to the wall beside the stairwell.

DO NOT ADMIT, was written above each face. Below each, *NOT A VOLUNTEER*.

"What does this mean?" Jonna asked.

"Oh," Marilyn said, letting out a huff of disgust. "Those are Human Firsters. They come here posing as volunteers, just to harass the aliens."

"You're kidding."

"Wish I were," Marilyn said. "You wonder why people take the time. Seems like they could be doing a lot more important things. But we've had a whole slew of them coming down here from different parts of the country, trying to infiltrate and cause trouble."

"What kind of trouble?"

"Yelling at them. *Go home!* As if they can. Sometimes hitting them. Even had one guy come in with a gun." Marilyn scoffed. "Doesn't watch the news, apparently."

Jonna nodded. Guns didn't work.

Clubs did. Rocks. Baseball bats. Fists. The news stories were replete with videos posted by proud patriots or appalled bystanders who did nothing to help the aliens, just filmed and screamed while someone beat the poor refugees to death.

Marilyn continued jogging up the stairs. Jonna hurried to keep up with her. Marilyn looked like she was in her seventies, but she had more energy than Jonna did at thirty-three.

Energy, passion, and a certain toughness Jonna always wished she could have. She admired old women —any women—who looked like they didn't put up with any bull.

Jonna liked to imagine herself as a woman like that. To think about what it would take. What changes she would make if she decided now, right now, to give up the scared, pushover version she had always been and start being someone else.

Cut her hair short. Stop wearing makeup. Stop dressing up to impress other people. Wear comfortable clothing and sneakers so she could run up stairs any time she needed to. Right now her wedge sandals and tight gray skirt were holding her back. She felt embarrassed to have been so vain.

Like anyone would care what she looked like in a place like this. What they wanted was her help.

"This is the men's side," Marilyn said, pointing down the long second-floor hallway. "Men and boys, as best as we can make out. Men with babies are down the other hall."

"Families?" Jonna asked.

"Very few," Marilyn said. "Those were the cots downstairs. Usually it's just one parent with one child."

"Where are the other—"

"Dead, I imagine," Marilyn said. "We aren't clear about that yet." She continued her brisk pace across the time-worn linoleum floor. "Infirmary," she said, pointing to each room in turn as she led Jonna through the second-floor maze. "Travel packs, all this row. We'll have you help with those on the women's floor upstairs. Clothes shops. They each get two outfits. People don't seem to want to see them without clothes, even though there's nothing to see."

Jonna paused briefly in each doorway. The rooms were tiny. Monk-sized. Filled to the ceiling with boxes and piles of clothing cast-offs from people who wanted to help however they could.

She had been one of those people up until recently. Dropping off donations in the parking lot of the monastery, then quickly driving away.

But yesterday, on her third such trip, something made her stay.

A yellow school bus had just pulled up, blocking all the parked cars, including Jonna's. She watched in her rear-view mirror, curious, dreading.

Two body-armored guards exited the bus and stood stationed in front of it, near the monastery doors. Both kept their hands on the clubs threaded through a loop on their weapons belts.

A stream of small gray-skinned beings, some of them no bigger than human toddlers, emerged from the yellow bus and flowed into the open doorway of the monastery. Most of them carried a baby or clutched the hand of a tiny child.

Jonna twisted around in her seat to watch them.

They all kept their long, oval-shaped heads angled down. No one made eye contact with the guards or the volunteers standing at the doorway to welcome them.

But Jonna felt the refugees. She *felt* them. Their pain and sorrow and fear. Their hope. Their longing. The wish by alien after alien as he or she filed into the building that this place would be good. That this place would be where they could stay.

That this place was finally safe.

One of them, one of the adults, if they were called that, stumbled getting out of the bus. The ARC guards stood impassive. One of the female volunteers rushed forward to help the alien to his or her legs.

The volunteer, a woman in her sixties, shot a look of such disgust to the guards, Jonna could feel her anger from the seat of her parked car twenty feet away.

She could also see that the guards not only didn't care, they almost enjoyed seeing the gray fluid running down the injured alien's leg.

They exchanged a smirking glance.

Jonna wanted to kick them.

When the last of the school bus was emptied, the guards got back inside and one of them took the wheel and drove away.

Jonna sat in her car, still twisted back and looking at the monastery door.

The clothing she had dropped off was ridiculous. Cute shorts and tees she thought she'd probably never miss. Even though she was slim, she was a giant compared to the aliens. They would all wear children's clothes. She didn't realize.

Now she knew, from Marilyn, that the monastery volunteers sorted through every item of clothes donated and gave away about eighty percent of it to other worthy charities. It was a win across the board, but it took time and effort to do the sorting.

Jonna was too embarrassed by her own misguided donations to wade through other people's mistakes.

So she had volunteered instead to help put together travel packs for the aliens for the next stage of their journey.

Marilyn strode to the end of the east-west hall and Jonna trotted after her. Again at the head of this second stairwell Jonna saw posters of people who weren't allowed, who weren't honest volunteers.

"I still don't understand," she said, looking at one of the pictures. The woman looked like she was in her late-forties. Long brown straggly hair. Plain-faced and earnest-looking in a way you'd expect her to be for the aliens, not part of the establishment against them.

Marilyn shrugged. "They're scared. Lot of people are. All we can do is try to educate them. Or ignore them and just keep doing what we're doing."

She jogged up the stairs to the third floor. Jonna did her best to keep up.

The smell was different here. Not the scent of the special foods cooking in the first-floor kitchen, or the musty odors from all the used clothing piled up in so many rooms, or even just the dank smell of an old building.

The third floor smelled like something more animal.

More pungent. Like a mixture of spoiled food and dirty litter boxes and stale sweat. Jonna winced as it hit her nose.

Marilyn didn't seem to notice the stench. She was probably used to it by now.

She opened a door and ushered Jonna inside the narrow room. Long tables had been set against three contiguous walls. Large, clear plastic bins were lined up on the tables. There were handwritten signs above each one.

Blankets.

Diapers.

Applesauce.

Sports Gel.

Water.

Jonna stared at the list for a moment. "So little," she murmured.

"But so much more than they came here with," Marilyn said. "These people—I keep doing that. These *aliens,*" she corrected herself, "have nothing. Whatever possessions they might have brought, ARC confiscates every last bit of it."

"Why?" Jonna asked.

"Think about it," said Marilyn. "All sorts of alien technology, right there for the grabbing. I imagine it goes straight to the military. Help them build new weapons." She shrugged. "Or maybe I'm cynical. Maybe it's to figure out how to make more advanced spaceships like these people have so we can travel as far as their planet some day. If it's still there. Who knows."

Jonna nodded. There was so much more to all of this than she ever imagined.

Marilyn pointed to the table on their left. "You'll start over here. Grab one of the backpacks. Load them in the order we have set up."

She demonstrated. On the ground was a box filled with new children's backpacks. Some of them had flowers on them, others had superheroes from the latest comic book-inspired movie.

"How did you get these?" Jonna asked.

"People do nice things," Marilyn said. "We get deliveries every day. Someone just sent us eighty new pairs of kids' sneakers, different sizes. Broke my heart, I was so grateful. These days, anytime someone does anything kind... That was cry number one, first thing this morning."

Jonna could feel her own eyes misting up.

"Don't start," said Marilyn, noticing. "You'll get me going again." The older woman cleared her throat. "Yesterday someone sent us five hundred new baby blankets. I'll have you pack some of those today."

"Wait, do they even need shoes?" Jonna asked, suddenly realizing what she had seen before. The aliens' slender legs ended in rounded stumps, not feet.

"No," Marilyn said, "but still, how nice. We sent them

on to a children's charity in Albuquerque. Those kids will be over the moon."

Marilyn raised an eyebrow. Her own choice of phrases hadn't escaped her notice.

The refugees were from somewhere over the moon. Past Mars, as best as the scientists could make out, maybe far past that, too. It was one of the many unknowns.

Yet known or not, these aliens were here and they were in desperate need of basic services and someplace to live.

Marilyn worked smoothly to load the supplies into the child-sized backpack. A yellow baby blanket with little white lambs on it. Two newborn-size disposable diapers.

"They don't defecate the way we do," she said as she loaded the diapers in. "You might have noticed a smell."

"I did," Jonna said, relieved to hear her say it out loud.

"It's a kind of secretion that comes through the infants' skin. But it's generally in the lower regions, and we figure the bus companies don't want any of that on their seats. So it's better to cover them up. It's hard to communicate to the parents why they should do it, but they seem to accept it."

Marilyn moved on to the snack-pack sizes of apple-sauce and loaded two into the backpack.

"How do they eat and drink?" Jonna asked. She had

seen their mouths. Mere horizontal slits at the lower part of their heads, no wider than a paperclip.

"Liquids," Marilyn said. "All liquids. Believe it or not, they take it in through those long fingers. Seems to absorb through their skin."

Jonna tried to picture it, but honestly couldn't. She thought of how elephants drank, sticking their trunks in the water and then slurping it from the trunks into their mouths.

But just absorbing it straight through their fingers…

"We have no idea what they ate on their planet," Marilyn said. "But we've tried a bunch of different things here, and the applesauce seems to work. Went like gang-busters. And the sports gels. Those seem popular. We've come up with our own variation that we can cook ourselves so we don't have to spend so much." She added two sports gels to the little backpack.

"The water," she said, moving on to the next bin. She let out a brief sigh. "This one was tricky. They can drink from plastic water bottles by sticking one of their fingers down into it, but their fingers are too long to twist open the caps. Someone else has to do it for them. And we can't really count on strangers."

Jonna felt a pang at that. She wanted to hope that she would help one of these refugees get a drink if they held out a bottle to her. But would she really? Maybe before today she would have been too scared. She would have gotten away as fast as she could.

"This is the best we can do," Marilyn said, holding up a tall silver insulated travel mug that Jonna normally associated with coffee.

"The opening is small," Marilyn said, demonstrating, "but most of them can squeeze a finger in." She slid open and closed the horizontal cover over the sip hole. "They can maneuver these fairly well."

She checked that the lid was secure, then tucked the mug inside the little backpack. She zipped the backpack closed and handed it to Jonna.

Jonna lifted it up and down by one of its straps, testing the weight.

"The water makes it heavy," Marilyn said, "but the adults are sturdier than they look. And we don't want to send them out there without at least some of the basics."

"Send them where?" Jonna asked. "Where do they go from here?"

The monastery was just a way-point. Temporary housing.

"All over," Marilyn said. "They can't leave here unless they have a sponsor. But there are people from Fresno to Portland to Atlanta. You name it. People really want to help. And face it, a lot of them are dying to meet an alien. See one for themselves."

Jonna could understand the curiosity. She felt it herself. Curiosity mixed with nervousness.

"So maybe we get in two hundred new refugees by

the end of today," Marilyn said, "but we're also sending a hundred or two out."

"How?" Jonna asked.

"We've got volunteers driving groups down to the bus station, morning to night."

Jonna thought what that must be like. A horrible image came to mind. "Then… do they just leave them there? To travel alone?"

"Have to," Marilyn said. "We can't send our people on every bus. The sponsor only pays for the refugee's ticket. But then someone will be there to pick them up at their destination."

"But if they're going far away," Jonna said. "They could be traveling for days."

"Usually," Marilyn agreed. "Some of the wealthier sponsors pay for plane tickets, but that's pretty rare."

"And there's no one to help them along the way?" Jonna asked, the shock of the whole situation starting to sink in. She could picture it, one of those small gray beings holding on to a tiny baby, riding a bus filled with human passengers, some of which were probably hostile. Maybe violent.

The refugees afraid, unable to communicate, confused about the customs of this strange, foreign planet.

Jonna felt a hard, sharp pain in her heart.

"It's not a good system," Marilyn said, giving her a

sad smile. "But it's the best we can do right now. The way the government is."

"But it's all so…" Jonna cleared her throat. She could feel a lump forming there again. She was determined not to cry. It would be easy to cry all day.

"It's tough," Marilyn said, clearly understanding. She patted Jonna on the back. "Come on now. Let's get you set up in here. I've got to go back downstairs and do a million things."

2

Jonna soon found a rhythm to packing the travel supplies. She made sure to check the lids to the water containers, just like Marilyn did, to ensure they stayed on tight inside the little backpacks. She hated to think of one of these poor refugees out there in the terrifying world and opening up the pack to find a wet blanket and wet diapers.

She couldn't imagine any of it, really. What she would do in similar circumstances. Could she be even half this brave? And to bring a baby with her? A little child? What would it be like to find herself completely stranded on a strange planet and have to rely on the kindness of another species?

It made her take extra care with each backpack she loaded. She folded the blankets neatly. Tucked the diapers against the sides so the food and the water could rest in between.

She wished she could give them something else. Even a toy. A memento. Something. But she also knew she couldn't load the packs any heavier. They would already be a burden for the aliens' small bodies.

There were other volunteers in other monk-sized rooms doing this same work, Jonna knew, but she was glad to be alone. There wasn't really enough space for two people amidst the tables and supplies, and it gave her a chance in the quiet to think about everything Marilyn had told her.

She just didn't know. Any of this. That's what she kept coming back to. The refugees had been streaming in and out of this monastery for the past three months, and Jonna had barely given them a thought.

Everyone knew about the Crisis. It filled some part of the news cycle every single day. The violence against them, the speculation—where did they really come from? Why so many at once? Did their planet blow up and they escaped? Or is this the first wave of aliens intent on colonizing Earth? Sob stories here and there of humans experiencing some bond with one of the refugees, saying into a camera, "They're just like us. They just want to live."

Jonna knew about some of it, generally, but overall it was too upsetting. Not just for her, but for so many. It was easier not to think about them. Not to hear too much. Until scientists really knew the answers, why just listen to all the wild guesses? It was better to wait and try to get on with normal life. Otherwise you're always living with the stress and dread. It was toxic.

Jonna only began bringing a few clothing donations because someone else from work talked about it. How it didn't take that much time, and she felt better after she did it, and really, doesn't everybody have a bunch of clothes they're never going to wear anymore? Why not donate them to a good cause?

But no one knew what was really going on in here.

If she had known—really known—Jonna would have come here sooner, she knew it. The way she felt now, the regret, the pain, she wished she had done something to help these poor aliens from the very first day.

When the last child-sized backpack was loaded and Jonna had stacked it neatly against the wall, she emerged from the monk's old bedroom to see what other work Marilyn had for her.

That was when she found the little mother out in the hallway all alone, pushing her baby in the doll-sized stroller.

Hungry.

"Yes. Let me show you where to go."

She beckoned to the mother, and then led her down the third-floor hallway.

Jonna could hear the wheels of the stroller scuffling along as they traveled right, then left, then right again.

She smelled that smell, the slightly animalistic odor, but it wasn't bad, just odd. She turned back often to make sure the mother was doing all right.

The eyes. Both hers and her baby's. Large black ovals, like thick ink drops that had run on a page.

But expressive. Even without eyebrows or any other way of changing the shape of her expression, the little mother looked up at Jonna with eyes that told a whole story.

Sadness, but mostly fear.

Desperate fear.

Jonna stopped in the middle of the hall and knelt down. The little mother pulled her stroller backward a few steps. Like a dog not sure whether this new person might hit it.

"We will help you," Jonna told her. "You're safe here. Do you understand *safe*?"

It was ridiculous, talking to this alien as if she could understand English.

Jonna closed her eyes and tried to think it. If she could feel the mother's thoughts, maybe the mother could feel hers.

Safe. Jonna tried to put the image in her mind of the little mother and her baby being cared for by the humans in this strange place. Of Marilyn handing her a blanket and offering her one of the cots. Of Jonna peeling open one of the applesauce containers and offering it for the mother to eat.

Jonna opened her eyes again. The alien looked at her with those bottomless black eyes and took a few steps forward again, pushing the stroller in front of her. The baby looked at Jonna, too, but in an unfocused way, as if this human was just part of the rest of the scenery.

"Come on," Jonna said to the mother. "You're hungry. We will feed you."

She tried to picture the sports gel and send the image to the mother.

Whether Jonna conveyed it adequately or not, the mother continued following her to the end of the hall.

At the top of the stairs, Jonna said, "Let me help you." But the little mother already had the stroller lifted high above her head, her thin gray arms taut, as she began descending on her slender footless legs.

As they passed the second floor, two other volunteers, both men, joined Jonna and the mother and her baby. Both carried armfuls of clothing. They said hello and hurried down the stairs.

Everyone here was faster than she was. Jonna needed to wear sneakers tomorrow, not these ridiculous wedges. She would do it all differently tomorrow. Dress like someone who was serious about being here to help.

When they reached the first floor, Jonna pointed down the long hall toward the dining area. The mother set the stroller back on the linoleum and hurried forward.

From behind her Jonna heard one of the volunteers call out, "New bus."

Jonna stayed with the mother and her baby. She didn't want to leave them alone to figure it out.

But the little mother wasn't going to be alone, Jonna soon saw. Far from it.

A few steps from the dining room, she would have sworn there was no one else in there. She didn't hear a sound.

But inside were at least two hundred, maybe more, of the small refugees, all of them being fed by smiling, silent workers.

As though the whole world had gone mute.

But somehow it didn't feel strange at all.

Jonna thought to the little mother, *"Here it is. Enjoy."*

The mother looked up at her with those liquid black eyes and Jonna could feel her relief.

Satisfied that the mother and her baby were in good hands, Jonna turned toward the door to leave.

Just then a sensation began to thrum through her body.

Like she was the string of an instrument that someone had just plucked.

Keeper.

The word—not the word, the *feeling* of that word—came into her mind from hundreds of voices.

Keeper, keeper, keeper!

Echoing into her bones.

There was an excitement in the room. Two hundred pairs of oval black eyes staring eagerly toward the doorway.

Jonna stared toward it, too. Certain that something of vital importance was about to come through.

Three new refugees entered the room. *Keeper, keeper.*

All eyes remained on the doorway.

Then a small gray alien entered alone.

The thrumming sped to a rapid buzz.

Jonna could hear it inside her ears, even though none of the refugees made any sound.

It reminded her of the buzzing static of the emergency broadcast signal that had blasted all over the country three months ago. For the first time in her life it didn't end with the phrase *"This is a test, this is only a test."*

There was movement throughout the dining area. The refugees began forming a single line. Mothers and fathers holding their babies or clasping the hands of their small gray children. All of them waiting their turn to shake hands, it looked like to Jonna, with the alien who had recently entered the room.

His right hand looked deformed. Injured. Like he couldn't open it all the way. Or maybe it was a she, Jonna couldn't tell. Marilyn was right, even though the refugees were all naked, there was nothing to see.

Jonna looked over at the other human volunteers in the room. They seemed as confused as she was about what was going on.

Jonna backed up against the wall so she could watch and give the refugees plenty of room.

She could see now that the new alien's hand was not as deformed as she originally thought. It did open slightly every time one of the other refugees reached out to press their small palms and long fingers against his.

During one of the exchanges, Jonna thought she saw something green inside the new alien's hand.

He wasn't deformed, he was holding something.

Something all of the other refugees wanted to touch.

Marilyn slipped into the room and came to stand next to Jonna. She, too, observed silently for a while. Jonna watched her face for some reaction.

At last it came, tears streaming down Marilyn's cheeks. The older woman pulled a wad of tissues out of her pocket and held them against her nose.

"What is it?" Jonna whispered.

Marilyn gulped a few times, obviously determined not to make any crying sounds. "It's a stone," she whispered. "One of their healing stones. Good for him—he must have sneaked it past the guards."

Keeper. Jonna understood it now.

This alien had been able to keep something.

She could see more of the object the harder she watched. It had a shape to it, though she couldn't tell what it was. And the stone was a soothing, bright green color with a thin band of yellow that streaked across its center.

It took some time, but finally every adult, baby, and child refugee in the dining room touched the stone in the Keeper's hand.

Then one of the refugees moved to the doorway and waited for the Keeper to follow.

"Come on," Marilyn whispered as the two aliens left the room. She motioned for some of the other volunteers to follow, too.

They all kept a quiet and respectful distance. "You'll see," Marilyn whispered, but Jonna thought she already knew where the refugee was leading the Keeper.

The two of them made the turn from the hallway into the room marked *Infirmary*.

Marilyn and Jonna and the other volunteers crowded around the doorway to watch.

There were ten blue cots packed together in the small room. Ten refugees lay in various ill and injured conditions.

The Keeper came to each bedside and pressed the stone to the aliens' hands.

Jonna saw a gash along one of their thin gray arms immediately seal up and disappear.

She drew in a breath. Tears pricked at her eyes. This was extraordinary. Something she wouldn't have believed if she didn't see it.

The kind of thing no one would believe if she told them.

Ashen-gray skin became what Jonna now knew to be the darker, healthier gray. A misshapen leg, obviously broken, straightened. Closed eyes opened. Aliens became well. Within ten minutes all ten of them were standing up from their cots.

The Keeper's escort now led him back to the door. Jonna and the other humans quickly stepped aside.

There were two more infirmaries on the upper two floors. Jonna watched as the Keeper and his escort journeyed toward the stairs.

Marilyn turned to Jonna with a broad smile and misty eyes.

"Do you see?" Marilyn asked.

Jonna nodded.

She saw.

She asked Marilyn for more work. Then she worked at it all day. Sorting clothing, packing backpacks, doing whatever task she could put her hands to.

More buses arrived. More refugees flowed in. Some left with the various volunteers who would drive them to the bus station.

It was Sunday. A day Jonna would normally spend doing laundry and cleaning her house. Grocery shopping. Watching TV. Spending time with her friends.

Now she sat on a shabby linoleum floor wearing sweat pants and lightly-used women's sneakers she fished out of the donated clothes. Her tight skirt and wedge sandals sat useless on top of her purse. She might donate them somewhere, not here, of course, but she felt like she never needed to wear them again.

Hungry. Sad. Afraid. As she walked the halls, as she did her work, she could feel the refugees' cries ringing against the bones of her ribs.

She tried to answer them back, each one of them. *You are welcome. You are safe. We will do whatever we can to help you.*

Jonna wasn't a child. She wasn't so naïve to think these refugees' journeys would be easy.

She wished she had the time and the money to accompany every one of them where they had to go.

Some of them would die. She knew that. Some of them would be hurt.

But it wasn't a reason not to try. To do everything that she could.

It was after six o'clock when Marilyn came to find her up on the third floor. Jonna had brought up another load of filled water bottles and was busy checking that the lids were tight.

"You can't work all night," Marilyn said. "You need rest. We all do."

"Just let me get a few more—"

"No," Marilyn said gently. "You have to trust me on this."

Jonna looked around the room, at all the tasks she

could still do. But maybe Marilyn was right. She should rest for the night and come back.

"I have to work until four tomorrow," she said. "But I can come back after that."

"Good," Marilyn said. "We'll take whatever you can give."

As the two of them walked down the various halls that led to the stairs, Jonna asked the question that had been occupying her mind.

"Will he leave the stone here? So you can use it even after he goes?"

"Would you?" Marilyn said. "Would you trust it to someone like us?"

Jonna thought about it. How she would feel if she were trapped as a refugee on another planet, and had antibiotics or some other healing medicine.

Would she hand it over to the aliens who lived there? Or would she hide it and keep it to herself? Knowing that she would still see more of her human comrades, and might need to heal some of them, too.

Jonna shook her head. "I wouldn't."

"Me either," Marilyn said. "But he'll help everyone who comes through here for the next few days, and that's a wonderful gift."

There was still enough daylight as Jonna left the monastery for her to see some of the activity around the parking lot.

Two SUVs and a minivan held the next group of refugees to be taken to the bus station.

At the side of one of the SUVs, a middle-aged heavyset male volunteer was just securing a child's booster seat inside the back. A small gray alien stood patiently waiting and holding a tiny baby to his or her chest.

The baby was wrapped in a thin, clean blanket. The alien wore a child-sized plain blue T-shirt and a pair of sagging pants. The hems of the pants were rolled up so the refugee wouldn't trip on the extra fabric.

The volunteer finished strapping in the booster seat, then set a little stool beside the door for the alien to climb. The alien crawled onto the seat and held the baby in position while the volunteer adjusted the seatbelt around them.

A few slightly larger refugees joined them and the volunteer strapped them in, too. Then the volunteer shut the doors to the SUV and walked around to the driver's side.

Jonna couldn't resist. She had to know. She hurried before the driver got in.

"How do you do it?" she asked him. "How can you just leave them? Doesn't it kill you?"

"Every time," he said. "Every day." He gave her a sad smile. "I've gotta go. I don't want them to miss their bus."

Jonna stepped back to watch the procession. Maybe

twenty refugees total would fit into those three roomy vehicles.

Twenty refugees on their way to an unfriendly bus station where they wouldn't be able to count on strangers to open their waters.

Jonna could feel the wave coming, rising thick inside her throat. She had to hold it back until the refugees left. She didn't want them to feel her grief.

She unlocked her car and slid inside.

Once she was sure they were far enough away, she bent her face to her hands and cried.

This was what she was afraid of. Not that they would hurt her or that it was dangerous somehow.

But that she would feel so much, just like this.

That she might feel helpless, seeing so much pain.

It was why she carried on with her life, just as it was, even though everyone knew the Crisis was real. That hordes of aliens had been crashing to Earth in their spaceships, emerging frightened with children in their arms.

It had to be so much worse where they had come from, for them to risk leaving it to come here. Here where the land and the people might be inhospitable. Where they knew no one and might never find help.

But Jonna would help them. Marilyn would help. Every volunteer who gave up their Sundays and their Saturdays and all the weeknights after work.

People who might quit their jobs for a while,

knowing the monastery would be available only three more months.

Jonna thought she might be one of them. She would look at her savings tonight and see.

Being here every day for now felt like the very least that she could do.

It was what she hoped some alien species would do for her if the roles were reversed.

She opened her glove box and found a travel pack of tissues. She used five to mop up her face.

Then she started her car. Drove away from this place.

Already hoping to return in the morning.

TIME MAP

TIME MAP

The handcuff on my right wrist was much tighter than it needed to be. I wasn't going anywhere. But I understood their need to assert some authority. The whole base was on high alert.

They had lost three priceless *assets*, as the people interrogating me kept calling them. I never corrected them. What would be the point? They didn't want my opinion, they didn't want my enlightened world view, they only wanted to know how I helped their assets escape. Right under their noses. No security cam footage, no clues, nothing.

They had me in one of the small concrete interview rooms, one-way mirror, just like in a TV cop show. The other half of the handcuff was attached to the leg of a gray metal table that was bolted into the floor.

I'd already been held for about three or four hours. There was no clock in the room, they took my watch, but you get a sense of blocks of time. They let me have one bathroom break, escorted by a guard, then back to the hard metal chair to wait and wait.

I was still in my blue coveralls and black work boots. No one took my shoelaces, so I guess they weren't worried I'd try to hang myself. From what? The table leg? I knew they were watching me through the glass. I just sat and thought my thoughts.

Mostly about how slick it all was. None of it my idea, which made it all the better. I could just shake my head at it and go along and watch the show unfold.

Plus I learned a lot in that last critical hour. Things I certainly never knew and didn't even suspect.

In the almost seven years I'd been there, you could say I befriended the guys. The *assets*. They were easy to like.

But before I got the job, I had to go through two weeks of psychological testing. I figured working as a civilian for the military, there would be all sorts of hurdles, but the psych questions were strange.

They showed me all sorts of pictures and videos of men, women, boys, and girls, all of every possible nationality and color.

They had me hooked up to sensors to see if I reacted negatively at all. Of course I didn't. I'm a black man, I've spent my life with prejudice, so you think I care if someone is Pakistani or Chinese or Native American? Come one, come all, I'll judge you by your actions. If you're an ass, you're an ass, I don't care what color you are. But if you're good people, then fine. Come sit by me.

And then, week two, they started slipping in some new kinds of pictures. People with horrible disfigurements. People who had obviously survived being burned. People who might have made a living with a traveling circus back in the old days, the only way they could support themselves.

And then, aliens. Cartoon aliens at first, little green Martians, then little gray extraterrestrials from science fiction movies.

Any reaction, Mr. Swan?

They checked my readouts. Didn't matter to me, green, gray, disfigured, any of it. I'd lived a life. I'd seen a lot of people.

Just to make sure I wasn't totally dead, they also showed me scenes from horror movies where face-eating aliens were stalking normal folk. I didn't care for those, because who would? They checked my readouts. Elevated heart rate, fast breathing, I guess they liked what they saw.

Because I got the job. Technician Specialist. Top security clearance.

I know I came highly recommended. My old boss at Champion Rigs must have known someone in the

Army, because they came looking for me, not the other way around. I didn't know their secret base in the wilderness outside Aspen, Colorado even existed.

The rules were strict. You live on base. You don't leave. You don't travel. We provide everything you need for free: food, comfortable housing, clothing, medical care, transportation, you name it.

I was recently out of a marriage and without a lot of personal prospects. I figured I'd take the job for a year or two, just to get my feet back under me. And learn some new things.

I've been what people call a mechanical wizard ever since I was a little boy. Not just normal fix-it and build-it kind of childhood play, but next level. When I was five I took apart my mother's vacuum and a few other appliances around the house, and used the parts to make a working spaceship for my plastic army men. I got it airborne. I've always been a nut about flight.

Teachers noticed me, they put me in programs. I won all sorts of competitions. Reggie Swan became a name. My picture in the paper, holding up those big fake checks that show thousands of dollars in prize money—that was me. I made a good living as a kid.

And just like basketball and football standouts who start getting scouted while they're still in junior high, my parents started getting offers early on. Scholarships to this college or that. High-paying tech jobs with Boeing and Ford and a lot of other companies. And military recruiters telling them why I'd do best in the Army, Air Force, or whoever that particular recruiter represented.

But I have a stubborn streak in me. A real obsession with not being bossed around. And I had a different plan in mind.

Learn everything. Try everything. Not the college route, that wasn't for me, but hands-on. Working cars and airplanes and ships for a while. Then bridges and high rises. Whatever someone could design and build, I wanted to have my hands on that. Learn how everything worked, down to the nuts and bolts and motors and rivets.

If you start at sixteen, like I did, you can work a lot of jobs by the time you're forty-six.

But I parked myself at Base X for six years and ten months—the longest I stayed anywhere—because there was more to learn there than anyplace else. I would have stayed there for the rest of my life if I could have kept learning from the guys.

When I finally got clearance to begin the job, the supervisor, Greg, took me to a special room for my orientation.

It was a little bigger than the one where they held me after they arrested me, but it had the same light gray concrete walls and metal table and metal chairs.

Greg said, "They tell me your psych eval was clean.

But I won't let you on the floor until I know you can handle it."

I had no idea what he was talking about. All they told me was I'd be working on high-tech flight simulators and maybe some special aircraft. It sounded interesting, but not something anyone would have to *handle.*

The door opened, a woman stepped through, and after her came three little kids.

I thought they were kids. But only for a half a second. Then the light in my brain went on …

Whoa.

They were about three feet tall. Hairless. Skin a pale pinkish-gray. Heads more of an oval shape than round.

Their eyes were gentle and beautiful. That was the first thing I thought. It took me a moment to realize how much larger they were than a human's. Maybe three times as large, and oval, and lidless. But the way they looked into my eyes, I just loved them right away.

I know that sounds strange for a grown man to say about extraterrestrials, but the bond was immediate. Like bonding with an animal just from the way it looks into your eyes.

You just *know.* You may be different species, but you are the same. You belong. The trust and the bond are real.

I smiled. I think I even laughed. But with a kind of wild joy that I got to see three such extraordinary beings.

My new supervisor was watching me closely all the time. He seemed relieved at my reaction.

I found out later there had been two other tech specialists before me who washed out the first time they met their new coworkers. Both of them freaked out so mightily, doctors had to come in and give them sedatives.

Then the techs were whisked off the base under all sort of security. I have no idea what happened to them after that.

Because they were risks now to the secret program on the base. They had seen and they couldn't unsee. They couldn't be allowed to talk about it, ever. The military has experience dealing with things like that.

But I wasn't going to be a problem. I was all in, from minute one.

The woman who had escorted the three extraterrestrials into the room introduced them as RJ, LX, and MT.

No kinds of names for friends. I renamed them RayJay, Linus, and Mit.

And finally I found out why I was there.

The three extraterrestrials—ETs, for easier reference —hadn't been captured, like I read might have happened back in the 1940s when spaceships started getting shot down in places like Roswell, New Mexico.

These three ETs had shown up on Base X voluntarily one day. Just out of the blue. I found out from talking to some of the officers that there have been all sorts of spaceships over the years hovering around military complexes, especially ones with nuclear weapons.

Like they're monitoring us. Trying to make sure these Neanderthals aren't blowing up their world like foolish teenagers playing around with gasoline and matches.

But RayJay and Linus and Mit didn't just buzz the base or disable the missiles, like some other ETs have done at other military installations. Instead, they came straight in one day, flying a disk-shaped craft with a glowing blue dome on top, and they landed on the airstrip right where any gawking personnel could see.

Communication was a challenge. It took a while to find someone suitable to act as interpreter.

It took a week, in fact, before they somehow found Kirsten Simmens, the woman who escorted them into the room the day I first met them.

She was an attractive young woman in her late twenties when I first met her, small, slender, with pale skin and long blonde hair. I don't know where they found her or how. There must be some kind of database, though, because her skills were perfectly suited to this case.

RayJay and the other two had small slits for mouths, but they didn't seem to have the mechanism for speech. No vocal cords. Nothing that allowed them to make any noise at all. I never heard them groan or laugh or cry. It would have been like trying to communicate with a fish.

They spoke with their eyes. They latched on with their gaze and you just knew what they were feeling. Sad, scared, frustrated, delighted—I felt many of their emotions over the years.

But Kirsten Simmens could do more than just feel what they felt. She could hear what they wanted to tell her.

It was at a particular frequency, she explained to me when she realized I was ready to learn how to do it myself. Like tuning in to a faint and secret radio station that you could only access if the ETs gave you a special dial.

Not everyone could hear them, even if they wanted to. RayJay and Linus and Mit were in charge. They decided who could hear them and couldn't.

And then when you did hear them—it made me laugh the first time. Because they were mimics. They talked to you in your own voice.

"Hey, Reggie?"

"Yeah, Reggie?"

That's what it sounded like. Like me having a conversation with myself in my own head.

Kirsten spent a lot of time with the three ETs and gained their trust. And the fact was, they wanted to be able to talk to someone. They had come to this planet and this particular base on purpose. It was no accident.

But they were new to the planet, obviously, and

didn't know which humans they should trust with their knowledge.

I came along two months after they'd already been there.

And I don't think it's an exaggeration to say I became their best friend.

They showed me. They taught me. They confided in me. Not just the mechanics of their spaceship that they intended to give to us humans.

They told me everything I asked. About themselves, about their people, about the planet that they came from, and their galaxy. All of it.

And they taught me how to build a spaceship like theirs. They taught me things maybe no other ET has shared with any other humans.

I learned how to easily create anti-gravity propulsion. How to make a ship invisible. How to pilot one without installing any levers or controls, but only by thinking to it with my mind.

RayJay told me he hadn't planned on sharing those extra details. He had specific instructions about how much to teach the Earthlings. He and the others were here to help us advance, as others like them had come before—many times over the millennia—but they were supposed to dole out just so much at a time. To keep our more primitive minds from overloading. And also to make sure we were using their technology for good, not to invent new ways of killing ourselves. We already had enough of those.

But RayJay could see that I was different. I could understand as much as he decided to teach me. And my heart is peaceful. I'm not a man of violence.

And RayJay knew that I loved him and Linus and Mit. He knew I would always protect them, I would never betray them, I only wanted what was best for them all the time.

I gave up caring about any of my old life. About anything outside the base. I didn't need anything but to work and to learn morning until night.

I would take the eleven o'clock bus back to my housing on base every night just so I could shower and sleep for a few hours, then I'd come right back on the first bus at six.

And I'd been living that way, loving every minute of my life, for the past almost seven years. My brain felt like it had grown ten times bigger than it ever was. I had learned so much about the universe and space travel and other life forms, I could write a hundred books on them to start and still have more to say.

But even the best things can't last. Think of your favorite dog or cat, dying too soon, when you wish they would live with you your whole life.

You still have all that love for them, you would still want them by your side even when you're an old, old man, but that isn't how life works. Even extraterrestrial life.

I could see that RayJay wasn't looking right for a while. His skin was losing the pink tint that always made all three of them look like they were blushing.

He was getting to be a duller and duller gray.

Finally I said, "RayJay, are you dying on me?"

He answered me in my own voice, speaking directly into my head. "Reggie, we have to go soon. Will you help us?"

We were alone in the special hangar where they kept the guys' ship. Only a few personnel were allowed to come in there.

So we were alone at the moment, just the four of us, and I bawled like a baby. I couldn't make myself stop.

I hugged RayJay. Then the other two guys came in for the hug, too, and we stood there, just clinging to each other like brothers who were about to be separated.

They didn't make any noise, but I could hear them inside my mind crying with the same sound I was making. Like hearing myself, and then three echoes of the same sobs. It made it so much worse to know that they were feeling it, too.

But then I got hold of myself. I said of course I'll help you however I can.

And then RayJay let me in on yet another secret. Of how I could help them escape.

I asked them to wait one more day. I wasn't ready to say goodbye. But I understood that RayJay needed to go back or he wasn't going to make it.

They told me they knew from the start that they would only stay for seven years. They had prepared their bodies to survive in our atmosphere for that long.

And they knew that I would be with them for almost all of those seven years.

"How did you know?"

"We saw you," came my own voice in my head. "On our time map."

They had hinted about their time map a few times before, but I never really understood what they meant.

"Do you mean time travel?" I asked them the first time, but they said it wasn't exactly that. "Is it a time machine?" I tried. "You see a time on your map and you can go there?"

But still the answer was no.

Now RayJay tried one more time to help me understand. He pressed one of his four pale gray fingers into his chest where a heart would be if he was a human instead of what he was.

Then he drew a line through the space between us, and pressed that same finger to where he knew my heart was.

"Beginning," said the Reggie voice in my mind, "end. Time to end of time."

"But you saw it," I said, trying to grasp what he

meant. "Like looking at a map, but not of a place. It was of a time."

I could feel RayJay smiling with his eyes. And I heard the rest of his explanation, and finally understood.

Before coming to Earth with Linus and Mit, they had looked at a time map to see when to come.

Just as they had consulted other maps to find the best location to bring their gift of technology to teach the humans. And just as other extraterrestrials before them had chosen the best time to bring their own earlier technology to humans living in earlier times.

Why are there suddenly a rash of discoveries and advances in different places around the world, all in the same few years?

Because the leaders of the ETs send out teams. They try to seed our planet with knowledge by sharing information with people they think can understand it. Little by little, bringing us children along. Helping us to do better. Helping us to understand the better and peaceful ways so maybe some day in the future we can join the greater unified community and not just try to shoot everybody who looks and sounds different.

So RayJay and the other two volunteered to be one of the teams. And they knew they had seven years to do as much as they could for as long as their bodies could survive. But which seven years should they use?

They saw me on their time map. Reginald Swan, making my way through a life as best as I could.

Not knowing I would get the job Base X. Not even dreaming I would one day meet RayJay and Linus and Mit.

But they knew. They saw it. Just like astronomers can map out the future paths of the stars.

So they landed when they did, and they waited for someone like Kirsten to come along to explain why they were here and what they intended to do.

And then they waited longer still, just a few more months, for their friend to show up, answering a job offer that didn't exist before they arrived.

I passed the psych test. I would accept people of all kind. I would accept aliens. I wouldn't freak out.

To the contrary, the minute I saw those three, it was like I'd come home to a planet I didn't know I had left.

And then all my lifelong mechanical wizardry finally had a reason to be.

If they had time, I wish they could have shown me how to make a time map of my own. To find out what to do next, now that they were leaving.

But there wasn't time. I could see that. RayJay had waited as long as he safely could.

Linus and Mit were still looking healthy to my eyes, but I knew they would soon look as gray and sickly as RayJay.

You have to let people go. Even if you don't want to. And I was ready to do whatever I could to help them.

So they gave me the one more day that I asked for,

and they told me as much as they could about whatever else I wanted to know.

Including how to help them escape. It took so little effort. That's why it worked so well.

They did not travel through the stars to get here to Earth. They didn't travel light years. They didn't travel distance.

They traveled time and dimension. Both of them entangled together. They slipped from their time and dimension into ours.

To our human sensibilities, they must have needed a spaceship to do it. And I spent the last seven years picking it apart and reverse-engineering it and learning about anti-gravity and all of its other special properties.

When they never needed the ship at all. And they proved it to me when they left.

They asked me to bring three items from my home. Small metal objects that were easy to conceal.

I plucked out three clean teaspoons from my kitchen drawer their last morning. And even though I was sad, desperately sad to know my friends were leaving, I still had to smile to myself at the absurdity of thinking these spoons were somehow going to transport them to a galaxy so far away.

I knew that whatever they were going to show me would be the last perfect lesson. But I couldn't even guess how it was all going to work out.

I dressed in my blue coveralls and heavy black work boots. I stuck the three spoons in my coveralls pocket.

I took the six o'clock bus. I didn't even pause at the commissary for my usual cup of coffee. I was too sad and nervous. I wanted both to delay it and to get it over with.

The three of them were waiting for me in the hangar beside their ship. The security cameras that monitored us at all times would have seen us greet each other and go inside the ship as we did almost every day.

There were no cameras inside the ship. There wasn't room and there wasn't a place to mount them. The interior walls were curved and smooth and there was barely space for the three small extraterrestrials and one five-foot-eight human.

I had to lie on my back, scrunched behind their command seats. But I loved it inside their ship and never minded the discomfort.

The walls always glowed with a faint kind of golden color, not metallic, but more like the first glow of sunrise.

It was always the perfect temperature, even though the hangar was too freezing in the winter and way too sweltering in the summer. Inside the craft it was always just right.

In the closed-in space I could smell the unique scent of the ETs. Both earthy and lemony. Like citrus-scented soil. I always wondered if they minded the way I smelled so sweaty at the end of a day. It was why I always wanted to shower at least once a day, to try to make it a little nicer for them.

But they never seemed offended by all the human aspects of me. They never minded any of my human failings.

My impatience when I wasn't learning as fast as I wanted, or when I couldn't easily understand what they were trying to say.

My anger sometimes at the way things were run on the base. The way people sometimes treated me like an underling to be bossed around.

My awkward, gangly physical form that couldn't copy their elegant motions with even a fraction of their finesse. Their ship was a work of art. Sometimes I felt like a gorilla trying to mimic the delicate work of their hands.

They forgave me all my failings. They embraced me as their brother.

And now it was time to say goodbye. I didn't even try to hold back my tears.

I pulled out the teaspoons from my pocket and gave them to RayJay. He handed one each to Linus and Mit.

Then RayJay struck his spoon against the smooth golden wall of his ship. I could hear a faint tinkling, like a vibrating chime.

Linus and Mit struck their spoons against the wall,

too, and RayJay said this was a resonance. The sound and vibration were all they needed.

I looked into their eyes. I could feel the love they felt for me. I know they could feel my love for them.

Then with the sound of three goodbyes in my head, all of them in my own voice, my teachers slipped away, like disappearing behind a hidden wall. One moment they were there, and the next the spoons fell with a ting to the floor of their craft and my three dearest friends were gone back to their homes.

I stayed there for a while. I couldn't bring myself to move. I cried like a boy who had just had to put down his beloved dog.

But I couldn't hide inside that spacecraft for very long. I had promised the guys I would cover their trail.

So I pulled myself together. I slapped my palms against my cheeks. I took some deep breaths. I had to do this right.

I climbed out of the craft like I'd done a hundred times before. No big deal, the ETs were obviously still inside working on something.

I went to the commissary and got myself a coffee and a danish. I made myself sit at one of the tables and take my time eating.

I went back to the hangar, knowing there were cameras that could confirm everything I did. I waved to where the guys would have been sitting inside their ship, and motioned that I just had to go do something first, and I'd be right back.

All to stretch out the time. All to confuse anyone who might try to piece together what had really happened.

Not that they could. I could barely understand it myself. But I promised the guys I would protect them all the way to the end.

I fiddled around at my locker for a little while, then I returned to the hangar and got ready to do the big act.

I climbed up to the ship and called out for RayJay. I opened it and looked inside.

Then I looked around the hangar and called to RayJay again.

I pretended to be puzzled. I started asking around. You seen the guys? Where could they be?

And then I saw Kirsten Simmens with her long blonde hair running through the door of the hangar, looking panicked.

She lived on the base, just like me, there to help facilitate communication with the ETs if anyone needed it. I don't know what she did most of the day, since I had no trouble talking to the guys myself and I never saw anyone else trying to talk to them separately.

Most everyone was afraid. They kept away. That was fine with RayJay and the guys. They had been told to be wary of most humans, and to try to find just a few who would understand them and want to help them, like Kirsten Simmens and me.

"Where are they?" Kirsten called to me. "They're not here!"

How she knew, I wasn't really sure.

She must have been locked onto their frequency even when she wasn't directly communicating with them. But whatever it was, she knew they were gone.

And then everybody knew. Kirsten made sure of that. I don't blame her, she was honestly upset.

And in time, just like I knew they would, the powers that be decided I had done something bad.

Four MPs showed up, ready to try to wrestle me to the ground. I held up my hands to show them I'd come willingly.

But they still cuffed my wrists before taking me on the perp walk across the base. And then they cuffed me to the heavy metal table in the interrogation room.

And for four hours I answered the same damn questions, posed by a parade of different people in charge: *What did you do with them? Where did you hide them?*

And then at some point they must have realized the ETs weren't hiding anywhere on base. Maybe because Kirsten Simmens said she couldn't sense them.

So then the questions were about how I helped them escape.

What could I say? That I gave them three spoons and *poof?* I said I had no idea where the guys were now. No reason to believe they escaped. They liked it here. Didn't we all treat them well? Why would they leave?

But no one seemed to be buying it. I was in trouble. Even though no one could prove I had any part of it. But I was the last one to see them, and that always means something.

So I sat there locked to the table and wondered how it was all going to sort out.

They took me to a cell eventually to sleep out the night. I lay on the hard bunk and stared up at the gray concrete ceiling.

I tried to imagine where RayJay and the guys were now. What they were doing. Where they lived. Who their people were.

How happy they all must have been to return to their home world. Even explorers eventually long for something familiar. Their favorite foods, their favorite places, the faces of people they love.

I wondered where I would go now. If I would ever return to my old life. Or if I was going to get disappeared like the two techs who washed out before me.

Or was I about to spend the rest of my life in some military prison?

If I had a time map of my own, I might have been able to see it.

But I guess smarter minds realized what they had in me. A man full of information and knowledge that shouldn't go to waste.

Locking me up in prison wouldn't help them create supertech spaceships of their own. What do we do with Reggie Swan? I became just another asset.

On my second day of interrogation I waited chained to the same gray metal table. I had a few bathroom breaks, escorted by a guard.

And then some time in the afternoon the door to the room opened again, and someone new came in, accompanied by Kirsten Simmens.

The man was shorter than me, maybe five-six, but buff and stocky, like he had been a wrestler back in his youth.

He was in his thirties, I guessed, white with brown hair and brown eyes. He wore a button-down shirt and a dark blue tie.

No jacket, so I could see the sweat stains in his pits. Maybe he had traveled all night to get to me and didn't have time to change his clothes.

He smiled at me and held out his hand. "Ted Whitling, Mr. Swan. Nice to meet you."

Kirsten took a seat and Whitling took the other. The three of us sat for a moment just judging what to do.

Kirsten had taught me where to find the right frequency to talk to the guys. But what I didn't realize was she and I could keep talking there even after they were gone.

I heard her in my head, talking in her own voice, not mine.

"He's from the government. One of their intelligence agencies. He's the one who found me and brought me here seven years ago. I think we can trust him."

"I don't trust anyone right now," I thought back to Kirsten. *"He's going to have to prove it."*

And it went on like that, with Ted Whitling talking to me out loud and Kirsten and I talking to each other in secret.

Whitling was different from the others. He didn't ask me any questions. Instead he spent his time telling me what he could do for me.

"I think you need to face something," he said. "This is the end of the road here." He looked at Kirsten. "For both of you. If you want to keep going, you have to pick a new road."

I wasn't sure what he meant by *keep going.* Was he telling us the military might decide to kill us for what we knew?

I had heard things. I wasn't happy to think it might happen to me, but I can't say I was surprised.

Or was Whitling just giving Kirsten Simmens and me career counseling? Telling us we were in dead-end jobs now and we needed to level up?

"Doing what?" I asked him. "What's the new road?"

Ted Whitling smiled. "I'd rather not discuss it here."

We were being watched and no doubt recorded. Whitling wasn't stupid. But neither am I, and I needed more than a vague promise.

Kirsten was young, but she had obviously learned a few things, too. She told me, *"We need some guarantee of our safety."*

"So, are we assets now, too?" I asked Whitling. "Are we being traded to someone else? Is that it, our lives aren't our own anymore?"

Whitling smiled. "Look, Mr. Swan. I'm going to be honest. I'm just a cog in a big machine, the same as you and Ms. Simmens. We aren't special. I'm afraid we can all be replaced. They just remove the defective part and stick another one in."

"I'm just a cog," I repeated.

"That's right," Whitling said. "So let's be smart about where we put you next."

Kirsten and I looked at each other.

I could see she didn't believe it any more than I did.

Not special? The hell with that. Kirsten Simmens and I were bright, shiny special if there ever was one. Both of us had just spent seven years getting to know three extraterrestrials. We couldn't just be plucked out and replaced by anyone else.

I don't know what RayJay and the others told Kirsten over that time, but they had sure filled my brain with exactly the kind of valuable information any government would want.

So I wasn't buying this idea that we were just replaceable cogs in a machine.

And it was time to make a deal that I wanted.

I have never been motivated by money or power. Those don't interest me in the least.

But everybody has their price.

All I've ever wanted since I was a little boy was to learn everything. Try everything. Know everything that there was to know.

What Ted Whitling should have said was the road stops here, and from now on you're cut off and you'll never learn the rest.

But I could see that on my own. And that was what I didn't want to lose. I wanted to take what RayJay, Linus, and Mit had taught me, and then keep going and going from there.

I couldn't speak for Kirsten Simmens, but if Whitling could find me a new place to slip in as a cog in the big machine, then as long as I could keep learning more, my answer was going to be yes.

But mindful of Kirsten, I said, "How are you going to guarantee our safety?"

"I'd like to discuss that with you," he said, "but not here."

I looked at Kirsten. She was chewing the side of her thumbnail. But her mind was working, too, even though she wasn't talking to me through all of the steps.

Maybe she, too, had no interest in returning to whatever her life had been before. How much work was there for extraterrestrial translators out in the regular world?

So both of us took Whitling's offer, not really knowing what it all meant.

But it was enough to know that he got them to take the handcuff off me right away. And that he and Kirsten and I would be leaving Base X on a jet within the hour.

I didn't bother going back to my place. I never really lived there, I lived for my work.

But Kirsten quickly packed a small bag and joined us as fast as she could.

Even though she still asked me, *"Do you think they're going to dispose of us?"*

I didn't think so, but how could I be sure?

But once we were in the air, jetting away from the base, Whitling took off his tie and visibly relaxed.

"Will you tell me how they did it?" he asked me. "How they got away?"

I thought about it, and told him maybe later, when I got to know him better.

If he wanted that from me, it was some leverage. I wasn't about to throw it away.

But the time came when I did tell him. That and a whole lot more.

It's been ten years now. Ten astonishing years. Years when I've gotten to make the most out of everything RayJay and the guys taught me.

All I can say is that I made the right choice. I can't speak for Kirsten, but she seems to be doing all right. They've even trained her to do more than just sit on the sidelines and wait for some extraterrestrials to show up needing a translator.

She goes out and finds them. She listens to the frequency in her head, and she knows where to go to greet them and show them to safety.

I told her that was what RayJay tried to teach me. About their time maps that told the extraterrestrials when to come.

How he drew a line from where his heart would have been if he were human, and drew it across the space between us to where my heart was.

I took it to mean he could feel me. Across the distances between our galaxies, on this planet where he intended to land.

He adjusted his travel for when he knew I would be here, ready to befriend him and learn everything he wanted to teach me.

"Maybe all of them have time maps," I told Kirsten. "And maybe the dot on some of their maps is *you*."

She's not the only one. There are people like Kirsten roaming all over the world right now, waiting to greet the teams that are coming to teach us.

"If you see RayJay," I told her. "Or Linus, or Mit..."

She gripped my arm and gave me a smile.

But I'm not counting on them coming back. They never said that they would.

Instead they taught me how to go and find them.

I've been working ten years on transportation of my

own. Not only building ships for the *machine*, as Ted Whitling called it, but also building one for me.

It's exactly like RayJay's, with smooth, curved walls inside that seem to glow golden like the first rays of sunrise.

The walls make a particular sound when you strike them with an ordinary metal teaspoon—one of the three that I saved from where they fell after the guys went away that day. Their spoons still vibrate at a particular frequency.

I've done tests. I've gone on short excursions.

And now it's time to go further afield.

But it isn't just the resonance or the sound or the vibration that take you there. It's also the time map you hold in your heart.

You reach out to someone on the other end. And when you find them, you lock on to the path you need to take.

Heart to heart across the galaxies. Back to the planet where you belong. At exactly the right time, so they're waiting for you there.

Tomorrow I'm leaving to go find my friends.

They're a dot on a time map, and my heart knows where to find them.

THE WINDS OF A YELLOW PLANET

1

Sharman Hix still wasn't sure about this. The fact that she had kept it secret from everybody else at the Factory had to be a sign. There was no question that technically she had sneaked the old man out.

But Major Fritz Zimholt had come willingly. Enthusiastically. Maybe even, Sharman was sorry to see, with a feeble kind of desperation.

She only hoped this journey wouldn't end in disappointment. Or worse, disaster.

She loved Fritz Zimholt. Loved him like a father. Over the fifteen years she had worked for him, piloting his experimental aircraft and training other pilots to fly, Sharman had come to think of Fritz as more than a boss, more even than a friend and mentor. He had replaced her family. Father, mother, and brother. Grandparents. The truth was, Fritz had been raising Sharman since she was eighteen. Whoever and whatever she was now, at thirty-three, she had Fritz to thank.

Sharman was already a pilot in high school. She had learned to fly through a program at her elementary school, back when she was only eleven. It was like putting on shoes that were perfectly and especially made for her. All of her flight instructors told Sharman she was a natural. But no one needed to tell her that. Sharman could already feel it from her very first flight. Like she had finally woken up in her right life.

She had her plan. College, advanced science degrees, Air Force, NASA. All on a path to become an astronaut.

Then Major Fritz Zimholt called her just a few days after she graduated from high school, and made her a better offer. A way to reach the stars much faster if she came to live at the Factory, Fritz's hidden facility in the mountains of Utah, to be a test pilot for him.

Best decision of Sharman's life. She couldn't even imagine what the past fifteen years would have been like outside in the regular world. She still missed her family at times—something she never admitted to a soul—but other than that, Sharman was exactly where she wanted to be.

But not if she was going to lose Fritz. Not this soon. He was only eighty-three. People were living past a hundred routinely now, weren't they? Why should Fritz be any different? Sharman still had so much to learn from him about so many things. It was all happening too fast. She wasn't ready.

Until just a few months ago, Sharman wouldn't have thought of Fritz as old. Mature, yes. Wise and experienced. But still hardy, still tall and imposing, still in command of his body and his mind.

Not anymore. His mind still seemed as sharp as ever—during the fewer and fewer hours he could stay awake—but Fritz's body was a mess. He wouldn't say what it was, but anyone with eyes could see. The dramatic weight loss, leaving his skin bagging on his arms and face. The strange chalky look of his skin. His sunken eyes. His halting gait. Loss of what remained of his white hair.

There were other signs, too, and they all added up. Fritz was dying. And maybe there was nothing anyone else could do.

But Sharman could do something. Maybe. How could she be sure? It was only an idea, a theory. Born of a wild and maybe irrational hope. But even though Fritz didn't say it, Sharman could see it in his reaction: What did he have to lose? What other options did he have?

If she could save him…

But if it didn't work, then he might die even sooner. Maybe even in the next hour.

Could Sharman stand to see that happen? To know that she was the one responsible?

But if she could save him...

Fritz dozed uneasily in the pilot's chair beside her. Sharman had watched the seat mold itself carefully around Fritz, the way it did around any pilot who sat there, but she thought maybe the pod took a little more time than usual. Maybe it sensed the pain in Fritz's bones. Sharman sent her pod a warm thought of gratitude. *Good boy.*

Sharman's relationship with her pod—her connection to it—had evolved over the past several years. She had always known it was alive and sentient, but she no longer thought of it as a temperamental horse she was learning to ride.

Now she knew it was part of her. An extension of her own body and mind. The man who had originally helped design the pods, Reggie Swan, taught Sharman to think of them as another layer of her own skin.

Sharman no longer needed the lighted circlet she used to wear around her head to communicate with her pod. She could do it easily now, just by tuning in to what she thought of as her pod's particular wavelength.

Once she saw that Fritz looked comfortably settled in the single seat, Sharman asked her pod to make more room and to create a seat for her. The pod smoothly expanded from its single-seater, spherical shape, into a double-wide with a second chair for Sharman. It also raised the dome above them to accommodate Fritz's height. Sharman and Fritz used to think the only people who could pilot the craft had to be small. Under about five foot-seven. But now they understood that the pods would adjust themselves to suit their favorite pilots and passengers. That included Fritz.

No matter what size the pod was, single or double or occasionally even larger, the inside of it was always cozy and sparse. There were no controls. No buttons to press. No levers to push or pull. The lower half of the pod looked gray from the outside, and the top half was a clear dome. The material it was made of rendered it invisible as it flew. Only Sharman's fellow pilots, wearing flight suits made of that same material, could recognize other pods in the air.

Sharman was wearing one of the special flight suits now, in her preferred color of matte gray. It was a nice muted color against her dark skin. She had never dressed for attention, not even when she was younger. She just wanted to study and learn and fly. Then and now.

Fritz wore a black flight suit that made him look like a scuba diver. He had the hood pulled up over his bald head and he wore the pliable black boots that were a standard part of the kit. Both of their flight suits fit them like a comfortable second skin and kept their bodies at a perfect temperature. And the material made the two of them as invisible as the ship. It was some kind of alien tech. Fritz had never told her more about it than that.

Sharman pulled up the thin hood of her suit and snugged it around her face. She tucked away the few stray curls of her short black hair. She reached down and removed her pliable black boots and stowed them at the side of the footwell. Then she settled into her seat.

As the chair began its process of molding around her, fitting her perfectly underneath her bent arms and around her torso and legs, Sharman spread her bare toes against the raised platform that angled toward her at the base of her feet. She liked to feel the pod, skin to skin. She always thought it made a better connection.

Sharman spoke inside her mind and gave her pod the coordinates of where she wanted to go. Then she added the step Reggie Swan had taught her when he came to visit several years ago. It was an advanced mental maneuver. Something Reggie said he learned from three extraterrestrial friends of his. He called it mental physics. A way that Sharman could tune her mind and heart into a kind of universal time map, to direct the craft straight where she wanted it to go without having to traverse any distance in space. They would arrive in an instant, like the snap of a rubber band.

Even though she knew the exact coordinates of the

spot where she wanted to take Fritz on the yellow planet, she wanted to let him see the whole planet first, from a distance, to take it all in.

Sharman knew Fritz was like her, always wanting to savor the wonder of a new experience. Fritz had a scientific, mechanical mind, but he was also a lover of beauty and the mysteries of the universe. She wouldn't cheat him of this.

"Fritz," she said gently. "Fritz. We're here."

The old man roused himself. He blinked a few times, trying to focus.

Then he pushed himself upright in his seat. A smile broke across his face. Sharman smiled just to see it.

Overall, the planet in front of them was a strange mustard yellow. It had darker patches in certain areas, dark brown, some of them black where a lava-like layer extended beneath some of the many dead volcanoes Sharman and her five-person crew had found here on their first visit just two days ago.

The planet had enough of an atmosphere that Sharman could see a thin film of cloud or mist in a section over to her right. Although considering the high winds on the planet surface, it could just as easily been pockets of dust storms or even tornadoes stirring up the powdery yellow dirt.

From here it was hard to see how rugged the surface of the planet was. A mixture of hard-packed dirt and rock, with a thick layer of loose, fine dust coating everything. The constant heavy winds kept the dust swirling and churning, reducing visibility to just a few feet in any direction.

Rising from the yellow, dusty plains were thousands of bare, rocky mountains. Interspersed among them were an equal number of dead volcanoes, some of which had once spewed their black lava across the plains and down into the valleys. If it had ever been habitable or hospitable, it certainly wasn't now. It was a dead planet covered with dead volcanoes.

A dead planet except for the one spot where Sharman was taking Fritz now.

Let him see for himself. Let him decide for himself. Sharman couldn't make that decision for him. Her whole plan involved a terrible level of risk. There was no guarantee it would work. No guarantee at all. In fact, there was probably only the slimmest chance that she could pull it off.

But they had come this far. She should at least show Fritz the place. If they turned around after that and went back to the Factory, no harm, no foul.

But if she lost her nerve now, she'd never forgive herself. Fritz should be the one to decide.

He stared out through the dome of the pod, surveying with apparent delight the mustard-colored planet before him. "What did you call it?" he asked.

The question surprised her. It wasn't Sharman's place to name the planets. That was for people on the science team. And as far as she knew, they were still calling it by a collection of letters and numbers. C5V-46. The plan was to come back here and map it, explore further over a series of more visits. But Sharman didn't want to wait for that. She saw what she saw. And immediately thought of Fritz.

"Why don't you name it?" she said. It seemed right that he should.

"I'll think of something," Fritz said. His eyelids made the kind of slow blink that signaled he might be falling asleep again. Sharman hated to see it. This vigorous man, so changed.

She needed to hurry up while he still had any energy to bring to the effort. Sharman couldn't see from here the place where she wanted to take him. And she didn't want to risk flying the pod through whatever that atmosphere below was made of. But she didn't have to. There was an easier way to do it.

Sharman knew the coordinates. She told her pod. It snapped them to the planet's surface.

The pod landed on a hard, flat plain where the yellow dust swarmed. The ferocious wind blew horizontally in this section and pelted the fine sand against the clear dome at the top of the pod. Sharman could feel the high winds rocking her craft. For the moment she stayed where she was.

Fritz had fallen asleep again, just in the silent space of the past few minutes. She felt reluctant to wake him.

Fritz's forehead was creased in a frown. Was he in pain? Having a nightmare? He moaned. That was enough. Sharman covered the top of his vein-lined hand with her own.

"Fritz?" she said softly. "We're here. Let's suit up and go out."

2

Their head gear was a strange piece designed by Reggie Swan. When Sharman first met Reggie, nine years ago, all she saw was a fit old black man, maybe in his seventies or so, with skin as dark as hers and a mass of hair threaded through with lots of gray. She had no idea at the time what a brilliant mind lay beneath those gray hairs.

Reggie brought a friend with him that first day.

Commander Sharman Hix. An older Sharman. Some future Sharman. Twenty-four-year-old Sharman got to meet her future self.

Older Sharman couldn't stay long, she had spaceship commanding to do—a fact that current Sharman still clung to and reminded herself of only about twenty times a day.

But Reggie Swan stayed on. He had a lot to discuss with Fritz. And in the almost year that he stayed, he taught Sharman a lot about the pods he had designed for Fritz back in the day.

Reggie also made some new equipment for the future work he knew Fritz and Sharman and others at the Factory would be doing one day.

And that equipment included the head gear Sharman helped Fritz put on and activate while they were still safely inside the pod.

Like the pods, the head gear was alive. Alive and thinking for itself.

It was made of the same clear material that formed the upper domes of the pods. It was transparent, light weight, unscratchable, unbreakable.

It took Sharman a while to understand that Reggie wasn't *building* with that material, wasn't constructing a piece of gear, he was *growing* it. Like cells in a Petri dish. Like the kind of spare body parts that could now be grown in laboratories just from the smallest sample of human tissue.

Reggie talked to his growing head gear. He talked through what exactly he wanted to accomplish. Something light weight, indestructible, and something that would mold itself to each individual wearer, the same way the pods' seats molded to the shape of their pilots.

It had to preserve life. It should maintain the perfect atmosphere inside the clear dome so that the person wearing it could breathe as easily as standing at sea level on Earth.

It had to keep out whatever noxious gases or choking atmosphere might surround the person on another planet, outside the pod, wherever they happened to be.

It had to provide superb visibility. In darkness, it lit up. In direct light, it darkened to protect the eyes.

In pelting dust storms, like this one, or in snow storms or rain or whatever might obscure the wearer's sight, the head gear shed the particles before they could accumulate.

Visibility might still be limited, like it was on the surface of the yellow planet, but only because the dust filled the air so thickly it was impossible to see more than a few feet ahead. But it wasn't the head gear's fault. Sharman never had to wipe her hand over it or shake the powdery dust off. Almost as soon as the dust touched the head gear, the material cleared it away.

And last, the head gear had to fit as comfortably as the flight suits. It had to fit slimly to the head—not a big bubble, like a helmet—so that the wearer could climb, run, even swim without ever having to worry about the head gear getting in the way or in any way holding them back.

And so what Sharman pressed against Fritz's forehead now was a simple gelatinous sheet of the thin, raw material. Like putting on a sticky note that covered the length of his face.

"Breathe," Sharman reminded him. "One breath in and out."

It was the out breath that mattered. The material took information from both the wearers' skin and from their exhalation. Fritz drew in a shallow breath and overemphasized the exhale. It made him start to cough. But the head gear didn't mind that. It was busy doing its work.

In half a minute it had constructed a protective sheath around Fritz's head. It was shaped to his individual features and sat just beyond the surface of his skin. Whatever filtering system Reggie had created, Sharman still didn't understand. All she knew was that there was plenty of room to breathe easily and she never felt like she was suffocating or overheating.

She applied one of the short ends of a second gelatinous sheet to her own forehead. She kept the hood of her flight suit in place, covering the back of her head and the edges of her face up to where the outside edges of her eyebrows began.

Sharman took a breath in and blew it out. The head gear grew into its finished form. Sharman took another few breaths, just to test it, although she knew by now that she could trust it. For all the head gear she had tested over the past several years, not a single one of them had failed.

Granted, most of the tests had been done while she was still flying in the Wasatch Mountain Range outside Salt Lake City. But she had tested it through wind and rain and snow, tested it at night and in bright sunlight. The head gear did what Reggie said it would do. Sharman had faith in the designer and in what he grew.

Sharman pulled her boots back on. Then she turned to Fritz and placed her hands on his shoulders. She looked him in the eyes.

"It's awful out there," she said. "The wind's going to knock you down. It almost carried me away."

Fritz smiled at that. Sharman was as petite as a pixie. But Fritz didn't say that a puff of air could carry her away.

Instead he nodded. He understood. He was letting her call the shots. It made Sharman feel strange. Strange and sad. Fritz should be in charge. But he couldn't be. Not the way he was now.

Maybe on the return trip. She hoped it with all of her heart.

"You hold my hand, understand? Never let go."

Fritz nodded. He wasn't smiling anymore. He looked tired. Tired and sick and worried. But also ready. Determined. He was with her. He wasn't backing down.

"Okay," Sharman said, "here we go."

The lid of the pod slicked back into the lower edge of the frame. Dust came storming into the craft.

"Make it fast!" Sharman shouted to be heard above

the wind. She helped Fritz climb out. He wasn't steady. She had to do a lot of the lifting.

She told the pod to close up, quickly. It slicked its dome lid up and over again. Sharman stood outside the pod gripping Fritz's hand tightly, holding him close against her side.

His grip was weak in return. His legs looked shaky. She had brought the pod as close to the phenomenon as she dared. She didn't want to risk landing on top of it.

One step, two, three, she had already paced it out a few days ago. Just ten steps. The wind beat against her body and her head. It wanted to get into her flight suit, into her eyes and mouth, but everything she wore held tight and kept the dust and pelting sand away.

There was no point in asking Fritz if he was doing all right. She would have had to shout it, and what if the answer was no? She was still going to keep dragging him forward, leaning into the ferocious wind. There was no going back. Not yet. Just a few more steps—

And then they entered the wind break that Sharman had found two days ago. Like pushing through a curtain hanging over a door to a place where suddenly everything was quiet and still.

Over on this side, the winds had other work to do. They couldn't waste time pummeling two puny humans who dared to intrude upon the planet.

In the sudden stillness, Sharman caught her breath. She could see Fritz's chest heaving. His hands and legs were trembling. Those ten arduous steps from the pod to here had taken all of his strength.

But he didn't seem to notice. Who could, in the face of what he saw?

Sharman watched Fritz as he watched the phenomenon. One cycle, a second, a third. Just to believe that what he saw was true. Sharman had watched it half a dozen times at first for that very same reason.

"Dear God," Fritz murmured.

Sharman answered, "I know."

3

On a dead yellow planet filled with dead volcanoes and dead bare mountains and plains covered in nothing but powdery yellow dust, there was, after all, life.

Right here, right where they stood. A patch of green as large as a soccer field. Green … sometimes.

A low shrub grew here. It had short, fleshy leaves, and small bulbous sacs that grew from the stalks and looked like they might contain water or some other liquid. Maybe only a few tablespoons per sac. Sharman hadn't dared pluck one or squeeze it to find out. She couldn't imagine interfering with the cycle.

If green plants grew here, it must mean there was water underground. But the green growing plants weren't her only clue.

The cycle progressed like this. The soil beneath the plants looked moist. Like someone had watered it lightly, for just a few minutes. Not long enough for the water to sink down, to penetrate. Just a little sprinkling.

The sprout of the plant emerged from the moist yellow soil. Very quickly. In maybe two or three seconds. It continued to grow upward, then outward, adding leaves, adding sacs. That took about five seconds. Maybe seven.

It reached its full height of about twelve inches. It was bushy by then, with lots of the little sacs. Call it another five to seven seconds.

Then the water at its base began to dry. The soil cracked. The plant died. Three seconds, maybe five. Very fast. Dead, it dried into a russet red. The sacs dried and burst open. Spores flew out. The circular winds carried the spores in a loop, where they fell upon the dry ground, then the ground moistened again, then a sprout came up, and the entire cycle repeated.

At most, from birth to death to rebirth, a cycle took about twenty-five to thirty seconds. Over and over. As the winds blew, carrying the spores or the seed pods or whatever the plant created. A whirlwind that produced life. Then death. But then life again, over and over.

Was it the wind or the plants? Sharman had watched the phenomenon as long as she could before the rest of her team returned. Somehow she didn't want to show them. Not yet. She didn't include it in her notes.

Because the idea had already come to her, come racing into her mind.

If she could bring Fritz here.

Let him somehow put himself in the way of those cycling winds.

It was crazy. But she couldn't shake the idea. She just knew it could be the answer.

So he was the first person who saw it, other than her. She didn't want to influence him. She needed to know his unfiltered thoughts.

"What do you think this is?" she asked.

Fritz watched another full cycle before he answered.

"I don't know," he said. "I'm not sure." He was still holding her hand. She could feel him shake.

She had to cut straight to it. They couldn't just stand here forever. "Is it the plants themselves or is it the wind?"

Fritz watched in silence two more cycles.

"The wind," he said. "The plants are trapped in it. If not for the wind, they would have died and dried up like everything else on this planet."

"Exactly," Sharman said. It was her analysis, too.

"And the moisture," Fritz said. "It wouldn't be there anymore. It would have dried up long ago. But somehow the wind keeps freshening it. Keeps it returning." He watched another cycle, then turned to Sharman. His eyes looked bright and alive. There was a new vigor in his expression.

"So tell me," he said. "What do you think I can do?"

"I … Fritz, I'm not sure about any of this."

"Understood."

Now that he was here, now that the moment was at hand, Sharman was afraid to commit. To suggest what she had in mind. She wanted it to come from him. She wanted it to be his idea.

And now she wondered whether she shouldn't have brought Caroline Baird along after all. She was Fritz's oldest friend at the Factory and she was his senior scientist. But Sharman felt certain that Caroline would have said not to do it. That it wouldn't work, that it wasn't what Sharman thought, it couldn't be the wind— all the objections had swirled in Sharman's head over the past two days, making her want to just sneak Fritz out on his own and see whether he thought it was anything that could help him, or whether the whole idea was too crazy.

"I think I would have to strip down," Fritz said. "Down to skin level."

So he was really thinking of doing it. He saw it the way she did.

"No head gear," she said. "I think you're right. And that's a whole separate risk. You can't breathe this air."

"But the cycle is fast," Fritz countered. "I can hold my breath that long."

"We don't know how the atmosphere might affect your skin," she countered. "What if it's poisonous?"

Their flight suits protected them from any of that. If Fritz was right—and Sharman thought he was, she'd had that same idea about him needing to strip down—then the risk of exposure might outweigh the so far very theoretical benefit of standing in the stream of that wind.

A lot to consider. And none of it guaranteed.

The temperature was bearable. Only about ninety-eight degrees. A mild summer afternoon where Sharman grew up in Phoenix, Arizona. So at least that shouldn't pose a problem.

"I don't know, Fritz. This has to be your decision. I'm not sure about any of it. This is all completely new."

"I don't have a lot of time for research," Fritz said. "As I'm sure you've guessed." He squeezed Sharman's hand. She squeezed his back.

"How do you think I should do it?" he asked. "Leave the head gear for last?"

"It all has to be fast," Sharman said. "Be ready to go right before the start of a new cycle. And the least possible exposure before that. I'll have to help you take it all off. But let's plan it first."

They agreed that for modesty's sake he would leave on his briefs. Maybe that was stupid, Sharman wasn't sure, but she couldn't make herself pretend that seeing her mentor and father figure naked was no big deal. It was.

But really, was it? If it meant the difference between him getting the full effects of the wind, or not?

Damn it, get over it. "Fritz, I think you have to strip down all the way. I won't look. Trust me."

Fritz nodded. Sharman thought maybe he was embarrassed, too. But they weren't children and this was too important to botch just because of her sense of modesty.

They rehearsed the sequence: the boots, the hood, the suit, the underwear, and last, quickly, the head gear.

Step into the stream of the wind at the very beginning of the cycle. Stand right over one of the plants. Arms extended from his sides to get maximum coverage against his skin. Hold his breath. Wait for the apex of when the other plants grew to their full height and width, then step out of the wind before it moved on to the death cycle, to the drying of the ground and the plants and the spreading of the spores.

"You have to get out of it in time," Sharman said. "You can't stay in there a half-second too long. You understand that, right?"

Fritz nodded. He was watching another cycle, no doubt trying to plan the right time to move in and the right time to escape. Like some action film where the hero had to rush between the spinning blades of an industrial fan to outrun the villain and not get sliced up in the process.

"Fritz…" Sharman waited until he gave her his attention. "I'm just not sure about any of this."

He smiled. A gentle, fatherly smile that was meant to reassure her. But there was a shadow behind his gaze that Sharman couldn't ignore.

He was sick. He was weak. He might be despairing of his chances back on Earth. Did that mean she should indulge him by throwing him into the blades of a spinning fan?

But why else had she brought him here? If there was a chance to save him, she had to try. Even if Caroline Baird or any other scientist or level-headed advisor might say this was the worst idea in the world.

Fritz had taken plenty of risks in his life. Sharman took them every day flying the experimental aircraft—and now spacecraft—that Fritz had developed in his mountain hideout. They were both brave and maybe foolish people, but it had gotten them this far. Standing on a dusty, windy yellow planet where there was still an oasis of life on this strange green sward.

"Let's get ready," Fritz said. He reached down and pulled off his boots. Sharman's heart started hammering. Her breath sped up. They were really going to do this. Oh, man.

Boots off, Fritz stood watching the middle of the current cycle. "Let's let a few more go by," he said. "Come on, though, let's hurry." He removed his head gear just long enough to pull down the hood of his flight suit. Head gear back on while he continued stripping the suit off his shoulders and chest.

Sharman helped him keep pulling it off. She peeled it like a used glove. She could turn it right side out again once he was out of it. For now they needed speed.

They stripped him completely naked. Sharman had no trouble averting her eyes. She knew she was being too sensitive. If she was a doctor or nurse, she wouldn't care.

Fritz was scrawnier than she knew. He had lost much more weight than she suspected when she saw him in his clothes. His skin looked papery and loose and an unhealthy shade of grayish-white. He didn't look strong at all anymore. He was a frail old man.

But frail or not, old or not, dying by the day, Fritz still stood upright and alert, feet poised to give him a running start, and he held his hand over his head gear, ready to strip that off last and run into the whirlwind.

"Let me count it," Sharman said. Her palms were sweating inside her suit. She stared at the nearest bush, the one where Fritz would run in and stand over. The bush was at its fullest point now. Any second it would begin to die back.

"Okay, get ready!" Sharman said. She gripped Fritz's arm, ready to launch him. "Mask off!" He stripped it away. "Almost! Okay, NOW!"

She pushed Fritz into the swirling wind. He strad-dled the bush and spread his arms.

Sharman's eyes jerked from Fritz to the plant beneath him, back to Fritz, back to the plant.

Moist soil. Fritz standing tall. Sprout popping up. Fritz. Now the leaves. The first few sacs. Then more. Fritz with his back to her, so she couldn't see his face, but he wasn't shaking anymore. He stood firm.

She couldn't risk calling out to him, asking if he was all right, asking what was happening. She didn't want to distract him, didn't want him to move. Not yet. It was almost time to jump out.

"Get ready!" she called. "Almost!" She didn't know if he could see the other plants from where he was looking. It might be her call alone. She had to get this right. She couldn't let Fritz stay a quarter-second too long and overstay the life cycle.

"Almost … NOW!" Sharman reached out and grabbed Fritz and yanked him out of the wind.

He bent over and braced his hands against his knees. He wheezed. He looked bad. He looked frightened. He looked shaken.

Sharman held the head gear back up to his face. It remolded itself around his head. Even without his hood and his flight suit on, the head gear sealed against his skin and reactivated so Fritz could breathe. He took several heaving breaths. Sharman didn't like the sound of any of them. And being exposed like this wasn't helping. She needed to get him suited up again.

"Fritz, we need to get you dressed." His eyes were wide, maybe panicked. But he nodded. He understood.

Sharman helped him with his briefs. It was hard for him to stand on one leg at a time. He leaned against her for support. Dressing him wasn't going to be easy.

The flight suit was skin tight. It wasn't something she could pull over his legs while he leaned against her. He would likely fall. He needed to put it on himself. But he didn't seem capable at the moment. This wasn't going to work. Sharman didn't know if Fritz was any better, or maybe even worse. She had to do what she could and then get him back to the pod.

"Just put on your boots," she told him. She helped him step into one at a time and pulled them up over his ankles. "Come on. Come with me." She grabbed his hand and carried his clothing under her opposite arm and pulled him back out into the ferocious horizontal wind.

After the quiet of the oasis, the noise was shocking and unnerving. The wind was at their backs going in this direction, but that didn't make it any easier. It pushed them, it pelted them with the fine yellow dust and obscured the view beyond just a foot in front of them. But it was just ten steps to the pod, ten plodding, difficult steps. Sharman called out to the pod with her mind and told it to get ready the moment it sensed her.

The pod waited until the last moment, then slid open for Sharman and Fritz to clamber back inside. The pod closed itself tight again. There was yellow dust all over the seats and the walls and the floor.

Fritz heaved a sigh and collapsed back against his seat. Sharman could see his thin chest rising and falling with each breath. He seemed as frail as ever. But then she raised her gaze to his eyes.

He was staring at her with an electric kind of intensity Sharman had never seen on his face before. As though some fire burned behind his brown irises, making them seem burnt orange around the black pupils.

"Fritz? Are you all right?" Sharman's voice sounded younger than she was anymore. But she knew it was because she was scared. She didn't know whether Fritz was well or closer to death. She gripped his hand. "Tell me!"

Fritz let out a throaty laugh. More like a bark than a man's laugh. He squeezed Sharman's hand. She could feel the strength returned to his fingers. She could feel the life flowing back into his veins.

There was color on his cheeks. Two high bright patches of rose, like he had a slight fever. His eyes looked brown again, not that strange fiery orange. For a moment he had looked possessed.

Fritz reached down and removed his boots again, then began pulling on his flight suit. As he did the words came tumbling out. Not halting, not weak, but strong and sure. "Yes, I'm all right. By God, I'm cured."

Sharman stared at him, wanting to believe it. Such a simple statement. *By God, I'm cured.*

"How do you know?" she asked anxiously. "How can you say that?" Her heart fluttered with a mixture of hope and fear. She didn't want Fritz to be wrong.

"It's not the wind," Fritz said. "We were wrong about that. Or at least it's not only the wind. That was time, Sharman. It's a loop of trapped time."

Sharman gave her head a sharp shake. Not from disbelief, but because she didn't understand.

Fritz finished pulling the flight suit up over his shoulders. He tugged the hood back over his bald head.

"What if we were caught in a loop right now?" Fritz said. "What if as soon as I finished dressing, I was naked again? And over and over I put on my flight suit, then it disappeared, then I put it on again. It would be because I'm caught in a time loop. The winds outside wouldn't have anything to do with it. In fact, now that I say it, it's clear that they're caught in that loop, too."

Now the light was dawning. Sharman took it from there.

"So the wind blows." She passed her hand from left to right in front of her in the pod. "Horizontally, just like the other wind we had fight through. But over there, in the oasis, let's call it, it returns to the left and blows right again. Over and over."

"Not a circle," Fritz confirmed. "We just assumed that because it makes sense from what we've seen before. We've never seen winds on Earth that blow in a repeating horizontal path."

"And so the plants," Sharman said. "They're caught in the loop, too. And the soil. All of it. A moment in time, but what … sped up?"

"Plants don't grow and die in half a minute," Fritz said. He shrugged. "Or maybe they do here. But whatever the time line was before, they all got trapped. They live and die over and over."

"And … so what does that mean for you?"

Fritz was silent for a moment. Sharman turned to stare out at the swirling yellow dust. This planet was inhospitable. It could not sustain life. At least not human life.

And yet it deserved investigation. Sharman still wanted to return here with her original crew. And maybe ask Caroline Baird to come, too. Let her see the oasis for herself.

But not until Fritz explained what happened to him. Sharman still didn't understand exactly what occurred. How could Fritz declare himself cured? It seemed too easy. Even though it was exactly what Sharman hoped would happen. She should be elated. And yet she still wasn't sure.

"Tell me what you noticed about the plants," Fritz said. "About the stages they went through in the cycle."

"I'm sure it's the same that you saw," she said. "They sprouted, they grew, they dried up and died, their dry spores went into the air and the sprouts grew from them again."

"Exactly," Fritz said. Then he waited. As if Sharman had just given herself the answer. But she still didn't understand it. She didn't have a clue.

"When did I join the cycle?" Fritz asked.

"Right at the beginning. Right when the soil looked moist. Before the sprouts came up."

"We timed it right," Fritz said. "*You* timed it right. You sent me in there just in the nick of time. What was my body when I entered the time loop?"

"Sick," Sharman said. "Dying."

"That was point zero," Fritz said. "So follow the line."

He drew a horizontal line through the air between them. Sharman stared at it, trying to solve the puzzle.

"Point zero," she said. "Sick. Point one, new life, sprouting from the soil."

"Where did that life start?" Fritz said. "It wasn't just the soil."

"No," Sharman said, "it was the spores."

"The dried, dead spores," Fritz said. "Carried on the wind back into the dry soil that was about to become wet."

Sharman closed her eyes and tried to see it. Tried to see the time loop of the plants and the soil and what it meant for Fritz.

"It's the death," she said. "Isn't it? That's where you came in, too."

"The dried, dead spore," Fritz said. "There just in time to catch life before it began again for every life form caught in the loop."

Sharman could see it in her mind. Fritz's body as the drifting spore. Showing up at the exact right moment, seeding the new plant just when the soil was ready to nourish it. If not for the death there would be no life.

Timing was everything. She had gotten lucky. A split second earlier or later, she would have missed it.

"So it cured you?" she asked. "How? It … grew a new you?"

"There was no death. You got me out in time. There was only life. The disease isn't here right now. It comes later." Fritz drew his finger across the air again. "Over here. But I never got there. You pulled me out in time."

Sharman took it in. It didn't make sense in her earthly world. But they weren't on Earth right now. And Reggie Swan had a theory that the physics on their home world might not be the same everywhere else. Maybe that was true of time. And of life and death, too.

There was no question that the man sitting beside her in the pod wasn't the same frail, sleepy old man she had brought out here. Fritz seemed vibrant again. Awake and alive. It wasn't her imagination. The change was real. Fritz felt it, too. Sharman was beginning to believe him.

Somehow she had found the exact right time in the

sequence. He didn't have to die to be reborn. Being close to death was near enough.

There was a lot Sharman still didn't understand about what had happened. But she had time now to figure it out. She wasn't racing to save Fritz's life.

"What are you going to call this place?" Sharman asked him. She sent a thought to her pod to take them home.

"You name it," Fritz told her. "You found it."

The pod snapped them back to the mountains of Utah, where the sky was blue, not swirling with yellow dust. Where the towering conifers and the wildflowers suddenly looked more vibrant and colorful than ever. Sharman feasted her eyes.

It was how she wanted to think of the yellow planet. Not the swirling dust, not the dead volcanoes, not the dry and dead yellow plains.

She wanted to celebrate the green patch of life she had found trapped in a pocket of wind. The patch of time trapped on the distant planet, endlessly restoring life from death.

"Let's call it Oasis," Sharman said.

Fritz smiled. She could tell he approved.

He had created a time loop of his own, whether he saw it that way or not. Fifteen years ago Fritz Zimholt had plucked a young pilot off the path she had planned to take, and instead brought her to this distant place to show her a bigger world.

A bigger universe. One she was learning to travel through now, using inventions her younger self never could have envisioned.

And today she had used her skills to bring Fritz to another planet where he could be healed. A completed loop.

Sharman would go back to Oasis. Soon. Maybe sometime in the next few days. Bring her team with her again. Learn more about the yellow world. Map it for future travelers who wanted to explore it for themselves.

But for now she just wanted to take Fritz home. He wasn't frail and exhausted anymore, but after all they had been through, both of them needed a rest.

But Sharman could already feel the urge to leave her home planet again. Maybe tomorrow. Travel outward and find out what else was there.

LOVE AND WAR

1

You could tell a person's age by their neck and their hands. Everything else had been plumped and smoothed with injections and sculpting and who knew what treatments were being offered these days, so that Lyrie's ninety-six-year-old client looked hardly any older than she was at thirty-six.

But his neck was a disaster. He wore turtleneck sweaters—exclusively, ridiculously, even in sweltering October heat—to hide the papery folds of skin on his neck, and gloves to try to hide the blue veins that inevitably popped out on old hands. Lyrie had seen those hands a few times now that the old man felt comfortable around her. It was too hard for him to sign mountains of documents with the gloves on, and now

that they were nearing the date of trial, he had mountains to sign.

Walter Merks was not Lyrie's first ultra-billionaire
client. She had grown accustomed to looking at their
plastic faces and insincere smiles and bright open eyes
that were surgicked that way. The current trend was a
pale blue eye that made them all look like dolls. Creepy,
but it was the unnaturalness of it that showed everyone
it must have cost a fortune. Next it would probably be
tails, with all the form-fitting pantsuits to go with them.
The way these people spent money never ceased to
amaze.

And one way they spent money—to the benefit of
Lyrie's bank account—was by hiring the top attorneys
at the most expensive law firms to play the system for
them whenever they were caught doing what they
shouldn't or had caught someone else doing it to them
first.

Walter and Claudette Merks had now sued each
other back and forth at least four or five times, not
counting their initial divorce, which went on for five
years. They must have developed a taste for it, because
ever since then one of them had sued the other at a rate
that kept them in court year after year after year.

Although Walter Merks didn't look any older for this
lawsuit than he did fifteen years ago during the divorce.
Lyrie had studied the recordings. Remarkable what the
modern health and vanity merchants could do.

Not to mention the availability on planets like Altaterra of hybrid plasma treatments using the exclusive alien composites pioneered by Walter Merks's own company, PlasMight. Walter Merks was its best advertisement. Everyone had seen the before and afters of Walter aging normally until around age forty, then once he made his discovery he suddenly regressed to look like a young man in his twenties. Smooth skin, thick dark hair, the flat stomach and rippling muscles of an athlete—which he was not and never had been. But money can buy you beauty. It had always been that way. And ever since his discovery, Walter had been slowly, slowly catching up to himself again. He swore that by age one hundred, he might look forty again. Maybe. But then who knew what his next century would look like. He planned to live forever.

But he still hadn't solved the problem with his neck and his hands. Whatever treatments he applied, they never completely did the trick. Old age still poked through.

"Walter, we need to focus. Stop with that."

He kept covering his left veiny hand with his right, trying not to look at it himself, let alone show Lyrie and her legal assistant Terese.

"Just keep signing," Lyrie said. "We're almost there."

Walter let out a breathy sigh. Here was another problem: his breath was no good. Both Lyrie and Terese leaned back from him in their own chairs on either side of him at the polished mahogany conference table. This was why Lyrie met with Walter in the law firm's fancy, oversized conference room rather than her equally fancy, oversized office. Once was enough. Then she knew. It took days for the stench of his breath and perspiration to go away, even though she had people from maintenance bring in fans and sprays and air cleaners. It didn't matter. The smell lingered on.

It had a pungent, fishy tang to it, probably from the kelp and fish oil pills and fish drinks that were all a rage these days. Not that anyone had seen a real fish or real kelp for years. But the nostalgia of it must have added to the mystique.

And there was no question it gave Walter's skin a moist, youthful glow, although it also made his skin look a little gray, like rotting meat, if anyone wanted to be honest. Lyrie kept it to herself. It wasn't her business. She just wanted to get through this.

So far she had spent five months on this case when it was supposed to be over in two. She had taken it on as a favor to one of her partners in the firm. He offered her whatever she wanted, *just please take this off my hands. Opposing counsel is killing me. Tell me what you want.*

Six weeks at the partner's estate in the Bahama Range? Free private space transport to any vacation destination of her choice? Hadn't she always talked about spending a winter at the Lunar Dunes? But nothing was as appealing as the deal Lyrie ultimately agreed to: no more divorce cases ever. That was the kind of freedom she really needed.

Walter and Claudette Merks's case wasn't technically a divorce, but dissolving one of their sub-corporations and dividing up the assets was close enough. It had all the sniping and personal attacks and far-too-intimate disclosures all of these ultra-billionaire domestic relations cases seemed to invite. No thank you. Lyrie became a lawyer to use her mind and her creativity, not to listen to tales of the weird among the over-privileged and often sick—in more ways than one—members of the highest upper class.

Every now and then she fantasized about chucking it all and going to work for one of the public defender offices. Any planet's would do. To actually meet real people who had real problems and to help them make something better of their lives. Not to help rich people stay enormously rich. The money and prestige of being a partner in Altaterra's most expensive and highly-rated firm weren't even a little interesting anymore. What Lyrie wanted was something meaty, something real.

Something right.

Helping Walter Merks hang on to more of his billions in this current battle against his ex was not exactly what Lyrie felt excited to get out of bed for anymore.

If not for...

Nope, not going to think it.

Irrelevant.

She would see him at trial, her first time since Joe packed up and left four years ago. She would be cordial. He would be cordial. Everyone here was an adult.

"Walter, focus."

Lyrie, focus.

Walter Merks flexed his veiny left hand with its bony left fingers and picked up the special marker again and signed, signed again, signed some more.

And if Lyrie's mind couldn't help but go there, to that face, that voice, his laugh, his smile, *his ... everything* —well...

The mind was a private place. No one needed to know.

2

J oe Taver fixed himself another cup of coffee from the automatic brewer on his credenza and stared out the fourteenth floor window through the steam from his mug. There were files he needed to review. Witnesses he needed to call. Notes to make, questions to prepare, strategies to consider.

His opponent would be doing the same. Count on it.

But for now he just needed a short break. Across the way on the roof of a neighboring mid-rise he could see the artificial winds blowing fat blossoms on the apple and cherry trees. A whole grove of them had been erected—not exactly planted, since they were fake—to compete with other roofs covered in artificial orange groves and mini-forests of aspens and pine trees. Grovesport had been voted the greenest urban outpost year after year. Businesses loved to build here where the subsidies made construction cheap and the lax business regulations made everyone prosper.

Joe usually worked from home. He rarely came into the office anymore. The views out the windows made him itch. At least that's what he told his partners. They laughed it off, attributed it to Joe's bizarre fascination with the natural world, and if he needed to feel real dirt between his hands to keep up his billable hours, then so be it. Work from home. Grow your own vegetables in that antiquated greenhouse. Pet your damn dog. Whatever it takes. Just keep on winning your cases.

So far that had never been a problem. Joe had a sharp legal mind. He got the job done.

But this case. He had to admit he was distracted. Seeing her name on every single court filing…

Lyrie Walsh.

Lyrie Walsh-Taver, if he had ever gotten his way.

But having a mother who married and divorced four men—maybe it was more by now, Joe didn't bother looking her up—had left its mark on Lyrie and had made her default answer no.

I love you, and no.

You're right, we're great together, and no.

I understand. I do. But … no.

Maybe it had been brinksmanship, gamesmanship, maybe it hadn't really been what was in his heart—Joe still questioned it sometimes when he dared to indulge in thoughts of her at all—but after eight years of loving her and being loved by her, it made no sense that she wouldn't make the commitment. So he left. Hoping—expecting—that it would all still work out if he did.

But Lyrie Walsh was as stubborn as he was. Or at least as he used to be. Time and more than a few blows had softened Joe's bull-headedness. He wasn't the man he was four years ago. Whether that was better or worse, wasn't for him to say.

Although he did wonder how Lyrie would see him now.

How could he not? The same way he kept thinking about what it would be like to see her in the flesh again. They had appeared on screen, both of them, during court hearings, but trials had to be in the flesh. An actual legal term, *in the flesh*, these days after the Altaterra Supreme Court ruled that holographic trials did not serve the public interest. If citizens wanted to avail themselves of the Altaterra court system, they had to put up with the expense and inconvenience of getting their butts to the planet and not just trying to shop around for the best and most sympathetic juries for their lavishly-produced trials.

Altaterra citizens surely did love a good show. And the wealth of the vacation homeowners there guaranteed top production value when they tried to prove their cases.

Joe's client, Claudette Merks, knew some of the top

producers in the entertainment business, and they were more than happy to spend her billions to create all the re-enactments and animation and graphics and light shows and soundtracks she needed to squeeze out her next installment of punishment from her sleezeball of an ex-husband.

Although as far as Joe could tell, Claudette was no prize herself. Not exactly the picture of a faithful, loving wife.

But everyone was entitled to a fair trial. And Joe Taver had a reputation as a fierce advocate with an inventive legal mind.

Joe drank down the last of his coffee. He needed to keep working the file. He might be known for his innovation and cleverness, but Lyrie Walsh was no lightweight. She always had more than a few tricks up her sleeve.

A faithful, loving wife.

A faithful, loving husband.

No point in thinking about any of it. The past was over.

But in just a week Joe would see her there, on Altaterra, in the flesh.

It did him no good to pretend he didn't care.

3

Lyrie liked to think of herself as practical. The way she managed her finances. The way she kept up her house. The way she bought her house in the first place, scanning the real estate listings day after day for years until she finally saw exactly what she wanted and pounced on it. The realtor joked that Lyrie must have had some kind of spyware on the realty company's computers, because he had barely just hit the button to post it when Lyrie's offer came speeding in.

When you know what you want, you don't hesitate.

At least, that was what the practical side of her said.

How many times had she watched her little sister hold back, wait, check out one more piece of research, ask one more person for advice—and then it was too late, the good thing was gone, never to return.

"Guess I wasn't meant to have it," Cyndy would say with a shrug. It drove Lyrie nuts.

"Or maybe you were meant to have it," she'd answer, trying to control her temper, "but you've convinced yourself you're not allowed."

They both grew up with the same mother. A mother who had no problem whatsoever taking exactly what she wanted, whether it was someone else's husband or a lover's lavish gifts or Lyrie's and Cyndy's education fund—*"I was going to put it back"*—and so many other entitlements Lyrie had stopped keeping count. Or keeping track of the money. At some point, early in her twenties when she figured out how to pay for law school herself, Lyrie had a very frank conversation with her little sister about where they actually stood with their mother.

"We can never count on her," Lyrie said. "In any way. She will always, always disappoint us. She may not realize she's lying when she promises something, but she is always lying."

Cyndy was only a teenager at the time and still believed it would all work out. And Lyrie did what she could to help her sister every single time their mother let her down.

"I'm not really made for college anyway," Cyndy said when they realized that her entire savings account was gone. But their mother got a fabulous tan that year thanks to the five cruises she took with her man of the moment. Lyrie tried not to remember any of their names. What was the point.

"You *are* made for it," she argued, but Cyndy was far too good-natured—a pushover—to take a stand. So even though she had an obvious aptitude for music and could have made a career of teaching and performing, Cyndy let it all go with the tides of the cruises and carved out a smaller life for herself moving from one insignificant job to another.

While Lyrie found her place at the best law firm in Altaterra and spent years climbing up that trellis, Cyndy zipped from one planet to another, one job, one little apartment after another, never quite settling down into a situation she found satisfying.

"She's not worth it," Lyrie said whenever Cyndy shared some latest sob story of their mother's about how this or that man had done her wrong. "Don't even listen."

"I feel sorry for her," Cyndy would say. "She never got over Dad."

I never got over Dad. But Lyrie kept that to herself. Cyndy was too young when he died to remember him, and too young to know that their mother's pitiful sorrow over him was no more than one of her shows.

Lyrie remembered all too well the temperature in the house whenever her father would come home. All her mother's laughter and cheeriness would instantly snap away. She might be playing with the girls one second, then the door opened and Lyrie's father came through, and all their mother did for the rest of the night was pick at him and criticize and ridicule and berate him.

Mostly on the topic of money. He never made enough. They never had enough. She married a lawyer, she reminded him, not a school teacher. He had tricked her. What was he doing wasting his life teaching remedial reading? It was absurd. He didn't care about her or his children. Didn't care that they had to live like this—which always confused Lyrie, because she loved their homey house—on and on until everyone went to bed.

When he died … when he died.

Her mother could cry all she wanted, but Lyrie knew she was really crying for herself. Not because she loved her husband and missed him. Not because her children would never see their father again. Lyrie's mother cried because now she had to figure it out, find someone else—which she did within six months.

Lyrie cracked another egg into her skillet. This was real life. Stop thinking about her irritating, pathetic mother.

It was nine o'clock at night, Lyrie still had work to do, but she had finally left the office an hour ago and realized when she walked through the door of her own homey house that she was starving. She scrounged up what she could find in the refrigerator and made herself scrambled eggs with mushrooms and Swiss cheese and a couple pieces of sourdough toast with strawberry jam from the farmers' market that delivered.

She plated her late dinner and took a few minutes to get out of her suit and into her soft clothes. This was real life.

Start thinking about Joe…

It wasn't a conscious decision, but there he was, vivid in her memories and her mind's eye.

She had a dream about him once, about a year after he left.

They were at a party somewhere, and a friend of theirs had just finished dancing with a scruffy, outdoorsy-looking man she had been flirting with for some time.

In the dream Lyrie leaned over to Joe and whispered, "Don't they look sweet together?"

Joe didn't answer right away. Then he said, "Do we look sweet together?"

Lyrie kissed him softly. "Of course. It's why I already married you."

She remembered waking up and feeling so sad about it. It had felt so real inside the dream. Talking to him, touching him, kissing him.

And what she said—that felt absolutely real. As if she had fallen into an alternate universe where that Lyrie had made a different choice.

Where that Joe had stuck around, and asked her one last time.

That was time she was going to say yes. She knew it. They just never got around to it.

Lyrie piled eggs onto her jam-smothered toast and took another bite. She sank back into her cushy dark blue sofa and tucked her plush white blanket around her feet. The night had cooled off and the house felt chilly, but she liked the feeling of being warm under a blanket on a cold night. It might feel even better with candles instead of overhead lights, but she was too comfortable to get up and go to the trouble.

And anyway, who was she kidding? She was never going to say yes to Joe, no matter how many times he asked her. Lyrie was her mother's worst critic. She would never ever follow in her mother's footsteps. "She runs everything through the man filter," Lyrie told her sister after one of the marriages failed, maybe the third one. "She never makes any decisions on her own. She can't imagine living without a man for even five seconds. Listen to me: Don't ever, ever be like that."

But Cyndy had a strand of their mother's restlessness inside her, and with every job change and planet move and any adjustment to her life, she found some new companion to try on with it, like switching wardrobes with the seasons.

Most of the guys weren't bad. Lyrie didn't mind any of them. But they weren't the One, Cyndy always admitted, then she switched up her life again and was off to try someone and something new.

Lyrie rested her empty plate on the table in front of her sofa. It was made of some kind of faux pine—real wood was beyond her means, even with the huge bonus she earned last year—but it did a good job of pretending to be what Lyrie remembered from their house in her childhood. Her father scoured garage sales and antique stores and brought home rare finds, like the child-sized rocking chair with the chipped paint on it that he stripped and refinished for four-year-old Cyndy. Their mother sold it along with most of their other furnishings the following year after Lyrie's father died. Lyrie still haunted the second-hand market and auction sites, hoping for a miracle one day when she might find that little rocker.

She liked to think of herself as practical, but in some ways that was a stretch. Truth was, she was intensely, abashedly sentimental.

"Do we look sweet together?"

"Of course. It's why I already married you."

Just a dream, but one she still remembered as if it were a real memory.

But it was as faux as all the faux wood in her house, there to make her feel cozy, there to allow her to pretend she wasn't living on the edge of a city full of conniving, narcissistic people who would scoff at the way she lived in her private life. This little cottage she made away from it all. A little cozy cabin she had been envisioning for years and years and waiting for something even slightly close to it to come onto the market.

Of course she had snatched it up. Even though the realtor admitted it needed a lot of work.

Lyrie only saw the potential. The beauty. She agreed it needed a *lot* of work, because why not get the best price she could? But in her heart she knew it needed very little renovation and just a whole lot of loving attention.

It was her escape. Her sanctuary. Maybe she did used to talk about vacations she wanted to go on, spending the winter in the Lunar Dunes, all of it. But once she found this house, she never needed to go or be anywhere else.

She had made herself a home.

By herself.

Here, alone with herself.

Lyrie shucked off the thought. It was coming in hard, trying to find a place to land.

Do we look sweet together?

Of course...

Shut it. Go take a shower. Early day tomorrow. You have a case to prepare.

4

Altaterra was a three and a half hour shuttle from Grovesport, and the whole journey was in the dark.

There were eight urban outposts at various distances from the planet, and the journey in always felt as subterranean as an old subway.

Joe packed as lightly as he could, but he still needed multiple suits and shirts for trial days, along with workout clothes (aspirational, in case he found himself with extra time, but he knew a morning jog would do him good and clear his head) and plain, normal clothes he could wear around the hotel. He would probably eat room service every night by the time he got back from court.

All of it standard, nothing he hadn't done multiple times in the last several years.

Just never against Lyrie. That was new.

There were ethical rules prohibiting spouses from representing opposing parties on a case, and occasionally there was some argument over whether that included former spouses—some of them *really* wanted to beat the other—but there were no rules saying former lovers couldn't represent opponents.

Even if they had lived together for eight years. Didn't matter as long as they never actually said the words and signed the paperwork to make it official.

When Joe took this case on, he knew his opponent was Lyrie's partner in her law firm, and that was all right. He had fought people at that firm before. But the day he got the notice that she had substituted in, he had to sit with that for a minute. Think about whether he should do anything about it.

But in the end he decided if she was all right with it, he was, too. Four years apart was a long time. He was different and she was probably different. Like one of their law school professors told them, litigation was all sharp elbows and hard heads. You're either cut out for it or you aren't. Joe and Lyrie were. They had both been at this a lot of years. The work was challenging, intellectually stimulating, and the battles weren't personal.

Usually.

Trial was set to begin in two days. The judge had

ordered the lawyers and their clients to appear for a mandatory settlement conference tomorrow morning. Standard, since most judges preferred not to actually have to work very hard. Especially in a place like Altaterra, where there were always so many better options for how to spend the days: skiing, scuba diving, paragliding, rock climbing, mountaineering, kayaking, sailing, windsurfing … the list went on. It was an outdoor paradise for people who had more money than they needed and who were healthy enough to keep playing hard, harder, hardest until finally their hybrid plasma treatments couldn't keep up with their chronological ages, or a parachute failed, or they slipped in the shower, or some other risk caught up with them.

Joe's client, Claudette Merks, was a youthful-looking sixty. Very youthful. Almost … frighteningly, bizarrely young-looking. She had waist-long thick golden hair she wore in a long ponytail, her legs had been sculpted and squeezed to look like they belonged to a prima ballerina, the muscles on her shoulders and arms made her seem like a champion swimmer, and yet her torso looked like it belonged to a fashion model who barely ate, except for the chest, which had clearly been enhanced. The shapes and sizes made no sense, geometrically and anatomically, but it was the fashion these days among the women of the elite. Joe found it generally repulsive.

Claudette had a habit of talking out of only the right

side of her mouth because some surgery last year had severed an important nerve on the left side, and even though Claudette had won millions in compensation and also had corrective surgery that completely cured the issue, she still didn't trust it, she told Joe when she first hired him, because if she overworked the nerve smiling or talking on that side, she might blow the circuit forever. Maybe it was a circuit. Joe wasn't sure. Maybe Claudette's whole face was one robotic circuit board operating to internal commands of smile, cry, speak.

She wasn't a terrible person, but she wasn't someone he wanted to spend a lot of time around, either. She offered to treat him to dinner tonight, but he passed. *"A lot to do to be ready for tomorrow."* What he most looked forward to was settling into his room and looking through some of the seed catalogs that had just come in. He wanted to plan his winter crop. More root vegetables this time, test out some of the heirloom varieties. Experiment with some hybrids. Plant some ornamentals. Generally stop working so many hours all year long, and instead watch things grow.

Joe knew his head wasn't in the game anymore. Another year, maybe. Two, at most. He was young to retire, but not too young to live in a different way. These last few years he had represented too many clients like Claudette Merks, spent too many weeks in hotels, wasted too many days arguing about legal issues that didn't interest him anymore.

There was a difference between things you could do and things you wanted to do. His partners would think he was crazy for giving up such a lucrative, high-profile career. But Joe was tired. He had lost too much lately and it was wearing on him.

Starting with giving up Lyrie four years ago. Maybe the biggest mistake of his life, or maybe inevitable. It was hard to say. There were two people in that equation, and both had an equal vote. But there was no question that was when the line of Joe's life started trending down.

But he didn't have to keep watching it all the way to the ground.

A crop fails, you plant a different crop.

You improve the soils. You change the watering. You figure out what went wrong and you fix it. There's always the next time. Until there isn't.

But there was a next time right now, in front of him. Seeing Lyrie Walsh tomorrow morning, in the flesh.

He could keep his head in the game for that.

5

If Lyrie slept an hour, she would have been surprised. Her eyeballs felt scratchy with fatigue. Her face looked blotchy in the mirror. A nice red swollen bag under her right eye.

Walter Merks probably had some product for that. BagAway, a Merks Company Innovation. Or he'd tell her to sit tight for half an hour while he pumped in a pint of his hybrid plasma, and she'd be looking eighteen again in no time.

She showered, drank a second cup of coffee, sat with her feet up on the coffee table looking out her window at what might someday be a garden. Right now it was dry, hard dirt, but it had potential. She could picture the rose bushes she wanted to plant there someday. White roses, like her father grew.

She did not want this day. If she could have put it off another ten years, she would have.

Truth was, she was ashamed.

All it would have taken was a simple card. A digital message. Some kind of acknowledgment of his loss.

She knew Joe's sister, of course she did. They had been friends for years. Sisters. Rebecca was much more like Lyrie than Lyrie's own sister was. They had the same viewpoint on so many topics. Including Joe.

They both loved him.

Word reached her slowly, about six months after it happened. Just a casual remark in a conversation with another lawyer. *You hear about Taver? Sister died in a crash. Heard he quit all his cases. Went off on some walkabout.*

Lyrie had barely held it together until she could get away and sob. It was so unfair. Rebecca was the kindest, the most lovable. She should have lived forever. What a terrible thing for Joe. He must be broken to pieces.

But he was off somewhere, and Lyrie didn't know what she should do. Time passed. Joe returned. Resumed his law practice. Resumed his life.

And it hung there in front of Lyrie: She should have said something. Done something. It was so wrong of her not to. So childish and selfish. They all loved each other. What was she doing?

And then it wasn't the right time anymore. Too late.

She should have reached out immediately, even if he didn't receive her message until he got back.

She thought about it on Rebecca's birthday. And then on Joe's. Back to Rebecca's, Joe's again … and still she did nothing, said nothing.

So what was she supposed to say today?

It was ridiculous, it was too late, but it was all she could think of.

Lyrie got up and searched through her cards. Chose one she hoped was right.

Then she pulled the blanket over herself on the sofa, put the card against her legal pad, picked up her pen and began to write.

6

Judge Biagosi might as well have brought in his golf clubs to go along with his outfit. He wasn't subtle at all. White pants, green polo shirt, the kind of shoes you change out of to get into your golf shoes. Clearly he would rather be out on the course at his club than stuck in his chambers at eight in the morning with a couple of lawyers and their difficult clients, all of them taking up the judge's valuable time.

"Let's get this over with," Judge Biagosi said. He snapped his fingers and held out his hand for the demand letters he wanted from each side.

Joe handed him the file folder. Lyrie was just reaching out with hers, and Joe caught it midway and added it to his. Just a polite gesture. He would probably do it for any opposing counsel.

Probably not.

He couldn't look at her. Not directly. The first sight of her when she walked through the door of the judge's chambers was enough.

It was as if he had just seen her the day before. No time in between. Her dark brown hair, slightly unruly, the way it curled in places around her face and made you look at her dark eyes and her high cheeks. The way her mouth could get so small when she was serious, like now, but when she smiled her whole face relaxed and you couldn't help but smile just to see it.

She wore black pants, a white shirt, black jacket. Very elegant, understated. Unlike Joe's client, whose lemon yellow skirt barely reached the top of her ballerina thighs, and her orange sleeveless top showed all her surgeons' talents in one glance.

Lyrie's client, Mr. Merks, was dressed only slightly more golfishly than the judge. Same kind of white pants, must be part of the golf uniform, and an orange turtleneck that looked like a matching set with his former wife's. Merks had added a jaunty white cap that made him look like he was already out on the links, ready to line up his putt.

For all Joe knew, Merks and the judge might be playing a round together later today. Judge Biagosi seemed like the type not to let a thing like ethics or the appearance of impropriety stand in the way of a good golf game.

Judge Biagosi studied the letters in both files. "Well, that's ridiculous," he muttered about something in Joe's. He smirked at most of Lyrie's.

Joe chanced glancing over at Lyrie. She was staring straight ahead, mouth small, very serious, watching the judge go through his motions.

"Your honor," she said, "if I may—"

Judge Biagosi held up his hand. He continued reading. Lyrie looked over at Joe. She made a face he recognized: *Unbelievable.*

Then she looked away again, as if she had let herself slip.

But just for that moment, to look into her dark eyes, to see her whole beautiful face, right there in the flesh—

Damn. He thought he was ready, but he wasn't.

"Plaintiffs," the judge said, "leave."

Joe stood and signaled for Claudette Merks to come with him. She huffed, as if being ordered to leave the room so abruptly were an insult, not just how these things were done.

"This might take a while," Joe told her as they walked down the hallway to a nearby conference room. But he was already getting a feeling about this. The judge's costume was certainly a clue.

Joe had crafted his demand letter with three separate parts: the big picture, the individual elements, and what he claimed was their bottom line. It was all part of the game. Claudette's bottom line was far lower, just as he assumed Lyrie's demand letter set out numbers that no one really believed were the real numbers.

These kinds of negotiations used to be part of the challenge. Part of the fun. Now they just bored him. All part of the endless parade of one meaningless case after another. People posturing and pretending. It was hard to remember why he ever liked it.

Joe really did know it was time to give it up. Let some bright-eyed young lawyer come into the law firm and take his place. Burnouts were usually at least fifty, but it happened when it happened. And no question, Joe was feeling burned to a crisp.

He heard a door open. Yep, this judge was on the fast track. Must have a start time before ten.

Lyrie stood in the doorway of the conference room. She jutted her right thumb over her shoulder. "You're up."

Walter Merks stuck his head in from behind her. "Pigs get fat, hogs get slaughtered," he told his ex-wife.

"Are you threatening me?" Claudette asked from the right side of her mouth.

"What I'm saying is be reasonable for the first time in your life. The jury's going to hate you. Look at you."

"That's enough," Joe said. He could see the hurt on Claudette's perfectly smooth face. Lyrie must have seen it, too, because she pulled Walter out of the room and scolded him, "Really?" as Joe gently escorted Claudette back down the hall.

Joe knew that tone so well. *Really?* Not putting up with Joe's or anyone else's nonsense. Like the expression she had shared with him back in chambers: *Unbelievable.* Two small moments from a time capsule. The Lyrie he used to know.

"Sit down," Judge Biagosi ordered. Joe and Claudette sat. The room smelled strangely fishy. Joe hadn't noticed that before.

The judge held a large red marker in his hand. He made a show of it: "No—" He crossed off a line of demands. "No—" Another one. "Yes," and he circled the acceptable terms. "Yes, but half," he said, circling another and putting a line through it.

He handed the letter back to Joe. "You have five minutes." The judge checked his watch. Nine o'clock tee time, for sure.

Joe and Claudette left the room.

The case was nearly settled.

Back to the conference room. Lyrie and Walter Merks sat talking about whatever they had to talk about.

Joe caught Lyrie's eye. "Can I speak to you?"

Claudette waited out in the hallway, uncertain where to go. She showed no inclination to enter the same room with her ex-husband.

Joe led her to the next conference room down the hallway, told her he would be back soon, then returned to where Lyrie still sat with Walter. This room smelled oddly fishy, too.

Walter handed Lyrie back their own red-marked demand letter, now with fresh black marks from his own pen. Lyrie passed the demand letter to Joe.

He scanned it. It wasn't ridiculous. It wasn't even unreasonable.

He took it down the hall to Claudette. This was how it was done. Months and even years of bitter fighting over every single aspect of a case, then fifteen or twenty minutes of *Okay, but seriously*, and a three-hundred-million-dollar lawsuit could settle just like that.

Back in the judge's chambers, it was only Joe and Lyrie this time. Their clients could pout or lick their wounds in their own separate rooms.

"So we done here?" Judge Biagosi said, already standing, already halfway to the door.

"Yes, your honor."

"Yes, your honor."

Lyrie handed him the final negotiated terms. Judge Biagosi waved them away. "Type them up and send them to my clerk. I'll get you the order later."

He was gone by the next heartbeat.

Joe and Lyrie stood alone.

Joe chuckled. "We did important work here today," he said, clearly meaning just the opposite.

"I feel heroic," Lyrie answered. She offered her hand. Joe shook it.

Her skin was warm. So was her gaze. Her mouth still looked small and serious, though. Her hand inside his felt tense.

She released her grip and took a half step back. Then she turned and removed something from her briefcase.

A pale blue envelope. Old fashioned, the kind that people used to use for birthday or greeting cards, back when people went to the trouble.

"I'll talk to you later, maybe," Lyrie said, and then she picked up her briefcase and left.

Joe held onto the envelope. She had written his name on the front. He recognized her handwriting. He wanted to open it, but not now. Not yet. Not with Claudette Merks still waiting for him in another room, waiting to be told they won—which they did, in a way, and so did Walter Merks, because that was how settlements went—and Joe needed to finish the job before he could satisfy his curiosity, which was scratching at him like a cat right now, scratching so hard he could feel it bleed. But he had to do this first.

"Claudette, congratulations," he told her, and despite her fear she smiled out of both sides of her mouth. Then she caught herself and her hand flew up to the left side and she pinned down her reckless lips.

She hugged Joe. Hard. "You're my favorite lawyer. I'll use you all the time now."

Is that a threat or a promise? But he didn't say it. She

was a nice enough lady. He wished her well. But no, he had no intention of ever representing her again.

Joe escorted his client out of the building and waited with her while the court valet brought her ride.

Then Joe found the nearest bench and sat and gave himself a few seconds more before he tore the seal on the envelope.

Because what was inside it might matter. It might hurt. It might not. He hadn't expected Lyrie to write him anything. But that, too, he remembered, was her way. Some things were too hard for her to say in person. She had written plenty of letters to her mother in the years he knew her, although Lyrie never let him read them and always tore them up rather than send them.

But she hadn't torn this one up. That had to count for something. Joe opened it and read.

Dear Joe,

Rebecca was the most wonderful person I ever met. She was a gift to this world and every world. It's the most terrible thing that she is gone. I know how much you loved her. I hope you know how much she loved you back. I have never seen a sister so proud of her big brother. You deserved it. You were so kind and loving to her. You did everything you should have done, without exception. You were the best brother she could ever have. I was a witness. I know.

There are so many things I am sorry for. If I start listing them, I might never stop.

But I am profoundly sorry that I left you alone with your grief. She was my sister, too. I should have said something. I should have helped you. I'm so sorry. It's unforgivable.

I want to hear about her. What I missed. Maybe no one wants to hear you talk about her, but I do.

If you want that, call me. If you don't want that, I understand. You owe me nothing. I owe you so much.

Lyrie

7

She wasn't sure what he would think. The transport dropped him off in front of her house and she watched him from inside, to see his reaction.

He had changed out of his lawyer clothes into jeans and a plain black T-shirt. So Joe. Not wanting to wear anyone's logo or anything uncomfortable or formal. Not in his private life.

Lyrie followed his gaze around the front of her yard. Tried to see it through his eyes: the faux wooden rail fence, the old-fashioned iron gate, the pots of petunias on her porch, the flower boxes beneath her windows filled with red and pink geraniums.

Lyrie knew what she saw in it when she first caught sight of the listing: *It's like a storybook cottage. I could live there. I could be happy there. Maybe get a dog someday. Sit in a chair by the window and read to my heart's content. Plant rose bushes. Bake bread.*

She didn't dare imagine more. That was like her mother, that was like Cyndy. Imagining it with someone by her side. Making that the most important piece of it. *Without a man, I'm nothing. Without a man, I'm miserable.* That was her mother, not Lyrie.

But out there, standing in front of her gate, was the one man she could imagine here. The one man she *had* imagined here. But Lyrie knew these past four years it was just a fantasy. She had botched it. There was no reason for him ever to want her back. *She* wouldn't want her back if she were in Joe's place.

Not because they weren't good together—they were. So good. That was the problem. She didn't blame Joe for not understanding. Lyrie wasn't sure now if she understood it herself. But if she were Joe Taver, she wouldn't trust Lyrie with her heart. Why should he? He had offered it to her again and again and all she could tell him was no.

Do we look sweet together?

Of course. It's why I already married you.

Lyrie heard the gate creak as Joe opened it. She liked that creak. It sounded real. This life she was making for herself was real.

Her own life, not her mother's. Why was she ever so afraid of that? Lyrie was nothing like her mother. She never had been.

She opened the door.

"Is this going to be awkward?" she asked Joe. "Or should we just forget all that?"

"Forget all that," he said, and true to his word, he took just a few more big steps to reach her, and then he folded her into his arms.

"Don't tell me all the things you're sorry for," he said. "We don't have time for that."

Lyrie lifted her chin from his chest. She looked up at that familiar face, at the lines that were new and that she wanted to trace with her fingers and memorize with her touch. She could pour out her heart to him now or over time. She was voting for the long haul.

"So we done here?" she asked, trying to sound like the impatient Judge Biagosi.

"Not even close," Joe answered, as he gathered her in closer and pressed his lips to hers.

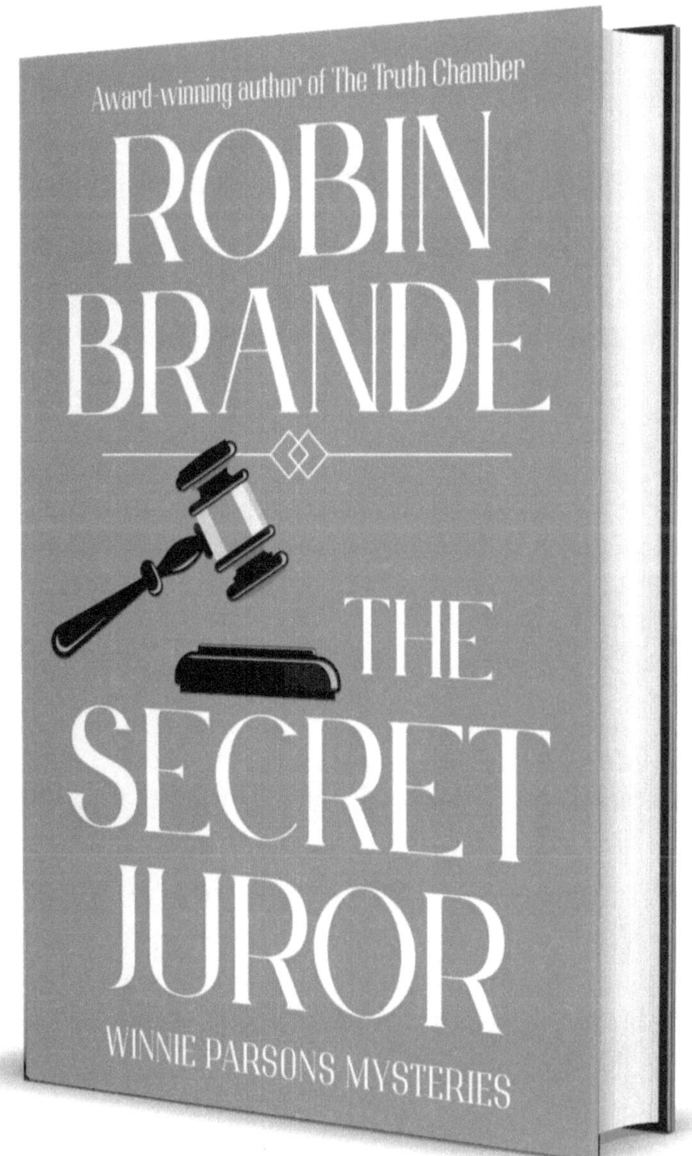

Liars can't hide
from Winnie Parsons.
But they sure keep trying.

The mind is a mysterious place. And the truth can change your life.

Stories of life after death, miracle healings, communication with other species, and more.

Open up your heart
to the love of a
good dog.

ABOUT THE AUTHOR

Robin Brande is an award-winning author, former trial attorney, black belt in martial arts, wilderness medic, and Reiki Master.

She writes in multiple genres, including mystery, fantasy, science fiction, young adult, romance, and self-help. She is also a designer and maker whose work celebrates the bookish life.

For more information:
robinbrande.com

www.ingramcontent.com/pod-product-compliance
Lightning Source LLC
Chambersburg PA
CBHW031751200726
48289CB00013B/773